B

M. C. BEATON

Death of a Gossip

A Hamish Macbeth Mystery

ENJOY ANOTHER HIGHLAND ADVENTURE!
LOOK FOR M. C. BEATON'S NEXT
HAMISH MACBETH MYSTERY

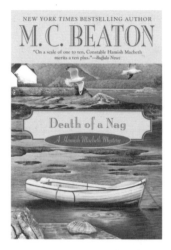

NEW YORK TIMES BESTSELLING AUTHOR

M. C. BEATON

"On a scale of one to ten, Constable Hamish Macbeth merits a ten plus."—*Buffalo News*

Death of a Nag

A Hamish Macbeth Mystery

Please turn to the back of the book for an excerpt.

ISBN 978-1-4555-0146-5

AND DON'T MISS THESE
OTHER NOVELS

NEW YORK TIMES BESTSELLER

M. C. BEATON

"On a scale of one to ten, Constable Hamish Macbeth merits a ten plus."—*Buffalo News*

Death of a Snob

A Hamish Macbeth Mystery

NEW YORK TIMES BESTSELLER

M. C. BEATON

"On a scale of one to ten, Constable Hamish Macbeth merits a ten plus."—*Buffalo News*

Death of a Hussy

A Hamish Macbeth Mystery

YOU MAY NEVER SPOT "NESSIE"
BUT YOU CAN STILL HAVE A MONSTER
OF A GOOD TIME WITH
M. C. BEATON'S

HIGHLAND MYSTERIES

Death *of a* Gossip

Previous Hamish Macbeth Mysteries by M. C. Beaton

M.C. BEATON

Death *of a* Gossip

GC

GRAND CENTRAL
PUBLISHING

NEW YORK　BOSTON

Grand Central Publishing
Hachette Book Group
1290 Avenue of the Americas
New York, NY 10104
www.HachetteBookGroup.com

Grand Central Publishing is a division of Hachette Book Group, Inc. The Grand Central Publishing name and logo is a trademark of Hachette Book Group, Inc.

The Hachette Speakers Bureau provides a wide range of authors for speaking events. To find out more, go to www.hachettespeakersbureau.com or call (866) 376-6591.

The publisher is not responsible for websites (or their content) that are not owned by the publisher.

Printed in the United States of America

First Grand Central Publishing mass market edition: February 1999
Reissued: August 2013

10 9 8 7 6 5 4 3

OPM

In memory of Fleet Street days—
for my very dear friend, Rita Marshall, with love

Cast of Characters
(in order of appearance)

John Cartwright: Owner of the Lochdubh School of Casting: Salmon and Trout Fishing

Heather Cartwright: His wife, and joint owner of the school

Marvin Roth: American businessman and budding congressman

Amy Roth: His wife

Lady Jane Winters: Society widow

Jeremy Blythe: Barrister from London

Alice Wilson: Secretary from London

Charlie Baxter: Twelve-year-old child from Manchester

Major Peter Frame: Ex-army, expert angler

Daphne Gore: Debutante from Oxford

Hamish Macbeth: Village constable

Priscilla Halburton-Smythe: Local landowner's daughter

Detective Chief Inspector Blair: Head of
    Strathbane CID
Detectives Jimmy Anderson and Harry McNab:
    Blair's assistants
John Harrington: Courting Priscilla
    Halburton-Smythe
Colonel and Mrs Halburton-Smythe: Priscilla's
    parents
Mr Johnson: Hotel manager
Angus MacGregor: Poacher

You came and quacked beside me in the wood,
You said: "The view from here is very good."
You said: "It's nice to be alone a bit."
And: "How the days are drawing out," you said.
By God—I wish—I wish that you were dead.

—RUPERT BROOKE

Day One

*Angling: incessant expectation, and perpetual
disappointment.*

—Arthur Young

"I hate the start of the week," said John Cartwright
fretfully. "Beginning with a new group. It's rather
like going on stage. Then I always feel I have to
apologize for being *English*. People who travel up
here to the wilds of Scotland expect to be instructed
by some great hairy Rob Roy, making jokes about
sax-pence and saying it's a braw bricht moonli-
cht nicht and lang may your lum reek and ghastly
things like that."

"Don't chatter," said his wife, Heather, placidly.
"It always works out all right. We've been running
this fishing school for three years and haven't had a
dissatisfied customer yet."

She looked at her husband with affection. John

Cartwright was small, thin, wiry, and nervous. He had sandy, wispy hair and rather prominent pale blue eyes. Heather had been one of his first pupils at the Lochdubh School of Casting: Salmon and Trout Fishing.

He had been seduced by the sight of her deft back cast and had only got around to discovering the other pleasures of her anatomy after they were married.

Heather was believed to be the better angler, although she tactfully hid her greater skill behind a pleasant motherly manner. Despite their vastly different temperaments, both Heather and John were dedicated, fanatical anglers.

Fishing was their hobby, their work, their obsession. Every week during the summer a new class would arrive at the Lochdubh Hotel. Rarely did they have a complete set of amateurs; experienced fishermen often joined the class, since they could fish excellent waters for reasonable rates. John would take care of the experts while Heather would mother the rank amateurs.

The class never consisted of more than ten. This week they had received two last-minute cancellations and so were expecting only eight.

"Now," muttered John, picking up a piece of paper, "I gather they all checked in at the hotel last night. There's an American couple from New York, Mr. and Mrs. Roth; a Lady Winters, widow of some Labour peer; Jeremy Blythe from London; Alice Wilson, also from London; Charlie Baxter, a twelve-year-old from Manchester—the kid's not living at the hotel, he's staying with an aunt in the village; Major Peter Frame. Oh dear, we had the galloping major before. These men who hang on to their army titles don't seem able to adapt to civilian life. Then there's Daphne Gore from Oxford. I'll send the major off on his own as soon as possible. Perhaps you'd better look after the kid."

John Cartwright glanced out of the hotel window and scowled. "Here comes our scrounging village constable. I told the hotel I needed coffee for eight people. But Hamish will just sit there like a dog until I give him some. Better phone down and tell them to set out an extra cup.

"What that policeman needs is a good, juicy murder. Keep him off our hands. All he's got to do all day is mooch around the village getting under everyone's feet. Jimmy, the water bailiff, told me the other day he thinks Hamish Macbeth *poaches.*"

"I doubt it," said Heather. "He's too lazy. He ought to get married. He must be all of thirty-five at least. Most of the girls in the village have broken their hearts over him at one time or another. I can't see the attraction."

She joined her husband at the window, and he put an arm around her plump shoulders. Hamish, Lochdubh's village constable, was strolling along the pier that lay outside the hotel, his hat pushed on the back of his head, and his hands in his pockets. He was very tall and thin and gawky. His uniform hung on his lanky frame, showing an expanse of bony wrist where the sleeves did not reach far enough and a length of woolly Argyll sock above large regulation boots. He removed his peaked hat and scratched his fiery red hair. Then he reached inside his tunic and thoughtfully scratched one armpit.

The smell of hot coffee wafted up from the hotel lounge below the Cartwrights' bedroom window. It obviously reached the nostrils of the policeman, for Hamish suddenly sniffed the air like a dog and then started to lope eagerly towards the hotel.

The Lochdubh Hotel had been built in the last century by the Duke of Anstey as one of his many country residences. It was battlemented and turreted like a castle. It had formal gardens at the back and the clear, limpid waters of Lochdubh at the front. It had stags' heads in the lounge, armoury in the hall, peat fires, and one of the best chefs in Scotland. Prices were astronomical, but the tourists came in droves, partly because the main road ended abruptly in front of the hotel, making it the only haven in a wilderness of barren moorland and towering mountains.

The village of Lochdubh nestled at the foot of two great peaks called the Two Sisters. It was a huddle of houses built in the eighteenth century to promote the fishing industry in the Highlands. The population had been declining steadily ever since.

There was a general store-cum-post office, a bakery, a craft shop and four churches, each with a congregation of about five.

The police station was one of the few modern buildings. The old police station had been a sort of damp hut. Constable Hamish Macbeth had arrived to take up his duties a year before the fishing school was established. No one knew quite how he had managed it, but, in no time at all, he had a trim new house built for himself with a modern office adjoining it with one cell. The former policeman had made his rounds on a bicycle. Constable Macbeth had prised a brand-new Morris out of the authorities. He kept chickens and geese and a large, slavering guard dog of indeterminate breed called Towser.

Lochdubh was situated in the far northwest of Scotland. In winter it went into a long hibernation.

In summer, the tourists brought it alive. The tourists were mostly English and were treated by the locals with outward Highland courtesy and inner Highland hate.

John Cartwright had been struggling for a month to make the fishing school pay when he had met Heather. It was Heather who had taken over the bookkeeping and put advertisements in the glossy magazines. It was Heather who had trebled John's low fees, pointing out shrewdly that people would pay up if they thought they were getting something exclusive and the rates were still reasonable considering the excellent salmon rivers they were allowed to fish. It was Heather who had made the whole thing work. She was plump, grey-haired, and motherly. Her marriage to John Cartwright was her second. John often thought he would never know what went on under his wife's placid brow, but he loved her as much as he loved angling, and sometimes, even uneasily, thought that the school would not have survived without her, although most of the time he prided himself on his business acumen and his wife comfortably did all she could to foster this belief.

He tugged on his old fishing jacket with its many pockets, picked up his notes, and looked nervously at his wife.

"Don't you think we should...well, meet them together?"

"You run along dear," said Heather. "Give me a shout when you're ready to show them the knots. Once you get started talking, you'll forget to be nervous."

John gave her a swift kiss on the cheek and made his way along to the main staircase. He prayed they would be a jolly crowd. At least he knew the major, although that was more a case of being comfortable with the evil he knew.

He pushed open the lounge door and blinked nervously at the eight people who were standing around eyeing each other warily. A bad sign. Usually by the time he put in his appearance, they had all introduced themselves.

Constable Hamish Macbeth was sitting in an armchair at the window, studying the *Daily Telegraph* crossword and whistling through his teeth in an irritating way.

John took a deep breath. Lights, camera, action. He was on.

"I think the first thing to do is to get acquainted," he said, smiling nervously at the silent group. "My name is John Cartwright, and I am your instructor. We find things go easier if we all get on a first-name basis. Now, who would like to start?"

"Start what?" demanded a heavyset woman imperiously.

"Hah, hah. Well, start introducing themselves."

"I'll be first," said an American voice. "My name is Marvin Roth, and this is my wife, Amy."

"I'm Daphne Gore," drawled a tall blonde, studying her fingernails.

"Jeremy Blythe." A handsome, stocky young man with a cheerful face, fair curly hair, and bright blue eyes.

"Charlie Baxter." The twelve-year-old. Chubby, beautiful skin, mop of black curls, remarkably cold and assessing eyes in one so young.

"Well, you know me. Major Peter Frame. Just call me Major. Everyone does." Small grey moustache in a thin, lined face; weak, petulant mouth; brand-new fishing clothes.

"Alice Wilson." Pretty, wholesome-looking girl; slight Liverpool accent, wrong clothes.

"I am Lady Jane Winters. You may call me Lady Jane. *Everyone* does." The heavyset woman. Heavy bust encased in silk blouse, heavy thighs bulging in knee breeches, fat calves in lovat wool stockings. Heavy fat face with large, heavy-lidded blue eyes. Small, sharp beak of a nose. Disappointed mouth.

"Now we've all got to know each other's names, we'll have some coffee," said John brightly.

Hamish uncoiled himself from the armchair and slouched forward.

Lady Jane eyed his approach with disfavour.

"Does the village constable take fishing lessons as well?" she demanded. Her voice was high and loud with a peculiarly grating edge to it.

"No, Mr. Macbeth often joins us on the first day for coffee."

"Why?" Lady Jane was standing with her hands on her hips between Hamish and the coffee table. The policeman craned his neck and looked over her fat shoulder at the coffee pot.

"Well," said John crossly, wishing Hamish would speak for himself. "We all like a cup of coffee and..."

"I do not pay taxes to entertain public servants," said Lady Jane. "Go about your business, Constable."

The policeman gazed down at her with a look of amiable stupidity in his hazel eyes. He made a move to step around her. Lady Jane blocked his path.

"Do you take your coffee regular, Officer?" asked Marvin Roth. He was a tall, pear-shaped man with a domed bald head and thick horn-rimmed glasses. He looked rather like the wealthy upper-eastside Americans portrayed in some *New Yorker* cartoons.

Hamish broke into speech for the first time. "I mostly take tea," he said in a soft Highland voice. "But I aye take the coffee when I get the chance."

"He means, do you take milk and sugar?" interposed John Cartwright, who had become used to translating Americanisms.

"Yes, thank you, sir," said Hamish. Lady Jane began to puff with outrage as Marvin poured a cup of coffee and handed it over her shoulder to the constable. Alice Wilson let out a nervous giggle and put her hand over her mouth to stifle it. Lady Jane gave her shoulders a massive shrug and sent the cup of coffee flying.

There was an awkward silence. Hamish picked up the cup from the floor and looked at it thoughtfully. He looked slowly and steadily at Lady Jane, who glared back at him triumphantly.

"Oh, *pullease* give the policeman his coffee," sighed Amy Roth. She was a well-preserved blonde with large, cow-like eyes, a heavy soft bosom, and surprisingly tough and wiry tennis-playing wrists.

"No," said Lady Jane stubbornly while John Cartwright flapped his notes and prayed for deliverance. Why wouldn't Hamish just *go*?

Lady Jane turned her back on Hamish and stared at Marvin as if defying him to pour any more coffee. Alice Wilson watched miserably. Why had she come on this awful holiday? It was costing so much, much more than she could afford.

But as she watched, she saw to her amazement the policeman had taken a sizeable chunk of Lady Jane's tightly clad bottom between thumb and fore-finger and was giving it a hearty pinch.

"You pinched my bum!" screamed Lady Jane.

"Och, no," said the policeman equably, moving past the outraged lady and pouring himself another cup of coffee. "It will be them Hielan midges. Teeth on them like the pterodactyls."

He ambled back to his armchair by the window and sat down, nursing his coffee cup.

"I shall write to that man's superior officer," muttered Lady Jane. "Is anyone going to pour?"

"I reckon we'll just help ourselves, honey," said Amy Roth sweetly.

Seeing that there was going to be no pleasant chatter over the cups, John Cartwright decided to begin his lecture.

Warming to his subject as he always did, he told them of the waters they would fish, of the habits of the elusive salmon, of the dos and don'ts, and then he handed around small plastic packets of thin transparent nylon cord.

He was about to call Heather down to tell her it was time to show the class how to tie a leader, when he suddenly felt he could not bear to see his wife humiliated by the terrible Lady Jane. She had been remarkably quiet during his lecture, but he felt sure she was only getting her second wind. He decided to go ahead on his own.

"I am now going to tell you how to tie a leader," he began.

"What on earth's a leader?" snapped Lady Jane.

"A leader," explained John, "is the thin, tapering piece of nylon which you attach to your line. A properly tapered leader, properly cast, deposits the fly lightly on the surface. The butt section of the leader, which is attached to the line, is only a bit less in diameter than the line. The next section is a little lighter, and so on down to the tippet. Now you must learn to tie these sections of leader together to form the tapering whole. The knot we use for this is called a blood knot. If you haven't tied this thin nylon before, you'll find it very difficult. So I'll pass around lengths of string for you to practice on."

"I saw some of these leader things already tapered in a fishing shop," said Lady Jane crossly. "So why do we have to waste a perfectly good morning sitting indoors tying knots like a lot of Boy Scouts?"

Heather's calm voice sounded from the doorway, and John heaved a sigh of relief.

"I am Heather Cartwright. Good morning, everybody. You were asking about leaders.

"Commercially tied leaders are obtainable in knotless forms," said Heather, advancing into the room. "You can buy them in lengths of seven and a half to twelve feet. But you will find the leader often gets broken above the tippet and so you will have to learn to tie it anyway. Now, watch closely and I'll show you how to do it. You can go off and fish the Marag if you want, Major," added Heather. "No need for you to sit through all this again."

"No experts in fly fishing," said the major heartily. "Always something to learn. I'll stay for a bit."

Alice Wilson wrestled with the knot. She would get one side of it right only to discover that the other side had miraculously unravelled itself.

The child, Charlie, was neatly tying knots as if he had fallen out of his cradle doing so. "Can you help me?" she whispered. "You're awfully good."

"No, I think that's cheating," said the child severely. "If you don't do it yourself, you'll never learn."

Alice blushed miserably. "I'll show you," said a pleasant voice on her other side. Alice found Jeremy Blythe surveying her sympathetically. He took the string from her and began to demonstrate.

After the class had been struggling for several

minutes, Heather said, "Have your leaders knotted by the time we set out tomorrow. Now if you will all go to your rooms and change, we'll meet back here in half an hour. John will take you up to the Marag and show you how to cast."

"Well, see you in half an hour," said Jeremy cheerfully. "Your name's Alice, isn't it?"

Alice nodded shyly. "And mine's Daphne," said a mocking voice at Jeremy's elbow, "or had you forgotten?"

"How could I?" said Jeremy. "We travelled up together on the same awful train."

They walked off arm in arm, and Alice felt even more miserable. For a moment she had hoped she would have a friend in Jeremy. But that fearfully sophisticated Daphne had quite obviously staked a claim on his attentions.

Lady Jane surveyed Alice's powder-blue Orlon trouser suit with pale, disapproving eyes. "I hope you've brought something suitable to wear," she said nastily. "You'll frighten the fish in that outfit."

Alice walked hurriedly away, not able to think of a suitable retort. Of course, she had thought of plenty by the time she reached the privacy of her bedroom, but then, that was always the way.

She looked at her reflection in the long glass in her hotel bedroom. The trouser suit had looked so bright and smart in London. Now it looked tawdry and cheap.

The stupid things one did for love, thought Alice miserably as she pulled out an old pair of corduroy trousers, an army sweater and Wellington boots, and prepared to change her clothes.

For Alice was secretary to Mr Thomas Patterson-James. Mr Patterson-James was chief accountant of Baxter and Berry, exporters and importers. He was forty-four, dark, and handsome—and married. And Alice loved him passionately.

He would tease her and ruffle her hair and call her "a little suburban miss," and Alice would smile adoringly back and wish she could become smart and fashionable.

Mr Patterson-James often let fall hints that his marriage was not a happy one. He had sighed over taking his annual vacation in Scotland but explained it was the done thing.

Everyone who was anyone, Alice gathered, went to Scotland in August to kill things. If you weren't slaughtering grouse, you were gaffing salmon.

So Alice had read an article about the fishing school in *The Field* and had promptly decided to go. She imagined the startled admiration on her boss's face when she casually described landing a twenty-pounder after a brutal fight.

Alice was nineteen years of age. She had fluffy fine brown hair and wide-spaced brown eyes. Her slim, almost boyish figure was her private despair.

She had once seen Mr. Patterson-James arm in arm with a busty blonde and wondered if the blonde were Mrs. Patterson-James.

It was not like being in the British Isles at all, thought Alice, looking out at the sun sparkling on the loch. The village was so tiny and the tracts of heather-covered moorland and weird twisted mountains so savage and primitive and vast.

Perhaps she would give it one more day and then go home. Would she get a refund? Alice's timid soul quailed at the idea of asking for money back. Surely only very common people did that.

Mr. Patterson-James was always describing people as common.

Suddenly she heard raised voices from the terrace below. Then loud and clear she heard Mr. Marvin Roth say savagely, "If she doesn't shut that goddamn mouth of hers, I'll shut it for her."

There was the sound of a door slamming and then silence.

Alice sat down on the bed, one leg in her trousers and one out. Her ideas of American men had been pretty much based on the works of P. G. Wodehouse. Men who looked like Marvin were supposed to be sweet and deferential to their wives, although they might belong to the class of Sing-Sing '45. Was everyone on this holiday going to be nasty? And whose mouth was going to be shut? Lady Jane's?

Jeremy Blythe seemed sweet. But the Daphnes of this world were always waiting around the corner to take away the nice men. Did Mrs. Patterson-James look like Daphne?

Alice gloomily surveyed her appearance in the glass when she had finished dressing. The corduroys fitted her slim hips snugly, and the bulky army sweater hid the deficiency of her bosom. Her Wellington boots were ... well, just Wellington boots.

Carefully setting a brand-new fishing hat of brown wool on top of her fluffy brown hair, Alice stuck her tongue out at her reflection and went out of her room and down the stairs, muttering, "I won't stay if I can't stand it."

To her surprise, everyone was dressed much the same as she was, with the exception of Lady Jane, who had simply changed her brogues for Wellingtons and was still wearing the breeches and blouse she had worn at the morning lecture.

"We'll all walk up to the Marag," said John Cartwright. "Heather will go ahead in the estate car with the rods and packed lunches."

Loch Marag, or the Marag as it was called by the

locals, was John's favorite training ground. It was a circular loch surrounded by pretty sylvan woodland. At one end it flowed out and down to the sea loch of Lochdubh in a series of waterfalls. It was amply stocked with trout and a fair number of salmon.

The major took himself cheerfully off to fish in the pool above the waterfall while the rest of the class gathered with their newly acquired rods at the shallow side of the loch to await instruction. Instead of a hook, a small piece of cotton wool was placed on the end of each leader.

It was then that the class discovered that Lady Jane was not only rude and aggressive, she was also incredibly clumsy.

Although the loch was only a short walk from the hotel, she had insisted on bringing her car and parking it at the edge of the loch. She backed it off the road onto the grass and right over the pile of packed lunches.

She refused to listen to John's careful instructions and whipped her line savagely back and forth, finally winding it around Marvin Roth's neck and nearly strangling him. She then strode into the water, failing to see small Charlie Baxter and sending him flying face down in the mud.

Charlie burst into tears and kicked Lady Jane in

the shins before Heather could scoop him up and drag him off.

"I'll kill her," muttered John. "She's ruining the holiday for everyone."

"Now, now," said Heather. "I'll deal with her while you look after the others."

Alice listened carefully as John Cartwright's now slightly shaking voice repeated the instructions.

"With the line in front of you, take a foot or so of the line from the reel with your left hand. Raise the rod, holding the wrist at a slight down slant. Bring the line off the water with a smooth motion but with enough power to send it behind you, stopping the rod at the twelve o'clock position. Your left hand holding the line pulls downwards. When the line has straightened out behind you, bring the rod forward smartly. As the line comes forward, follow through to the ten o'clock position, letting the line fall gently to the water. Oh, *very* good, Alice."

Alice flushed with pleasure. Heather had said something to Lady Jane, and Lady Jane had stalked off. Without her overbearing presence, the day seemed to take on light and colour. Heather shouted she was returning to the hotel to bring back more packed lunches.

A buzzard sailed above in the light blue sky. Enormous clumps of purple heather studied their reflections in the mirror surface of the loch. The peaty water danced as Alice waded dreamily in the red and gold shallows, which sparkled and glittered like marcasite. She cast, and cast, and cast again until her arms ached. Heather came back with new lunches, and they all gathered around the estate car, with the exception of Lady Jane and the major.

Suddenly, it *was* a holiday. A damp and scrubbed Charlie had been brought back by Heather. He sat with his back against the estate car's wheel contentedly munching a sandwich.

All at once he said in his clear treble, "That is quite a frightful woman, you know."

No one said, "Who?"

Although no one added their criticism to Charlie's, they were all bonded together in a common resentment against Lady Jane and an equally common determination that she was not going to spoil things.

"Oh, there's Constable Macbeth," said Alice.

The lanky figure of the policeman had materialized behind the group.

"Those sandwiches look very good," he said, studying the sky.

"Help yourself," said Heather, rather crossly. "Packed lunches are not all that expensive, Mr Macbeth."

"Is that a fact," said the constable pleasantly. "I'm right glad to hear it. I would not want to be taking away food that cost a lot."

To Alice's amusement, he produced a small collapsible plastic cup from the inside of his tunic and held it out to Heather, who muttered something under her breath as she filled it up with tea.

"You obviously don't get much crime in this area, Officer," said Daphne caustically.

"I wouldnae say that," said Hamish between bites of ham sandwich. "People are awfy wicked. The drunkenness on a Saturday night is a fair disgrace."

"Have you made any major arrests?" pursued Daphne, catching Jeremy Blythe's eye and inviting him to share in the baiting of Hamish.

"No, I hivnae bagged any majors. A few sodjers sometimes."

Amy Roth let out a trill of laughter, and Daphne said crossly to Hamish, "Are you being deliberately stupid?"

Hamish looked horrified. "I would no more dream of being deliberately stupid, miss, than you yourself would dream of being deliberately bitchy."

"Fun's over," whispered Jeremy to Alice. "Back comes Lady Jane."

She came crashing through the undergrowth. Her broad face was flushed, and she had a scratch down one cheek. But her eyes held a triumphant, satisfied gleam.

John Cartwright hurriedly began to make arrangements to move his school on to further fishing grounds for the afternoon. Boxes of hooks were distributed. More knots demonstrated—a towel knot and a figure of eight.

This time even Lady Jane struggled away in silence to master the slippery nylon. The fever of catching fish was upon the little party.

"Now," said Heather, "we'll issue you each with knotted leaders, but have your own leaders knotted and ready for tomorrow morning. We have the Anstey River for the afternoon. Carry this fishing permit—I'll give you each one—in your pockets in case you are stopped by the water bailiffs. Marvin and Amy, I believe you have done some fly fishing in the States. We'll start you off on the upper beats. We suggest you keep moving. Never fish in one spot for too long. If you come back to the hotel before we set out, then we'll issue you with waders. John and I will show each of you what to do as soon as we're on the river. We'll need to take the cars. John and I will take Alice and Charlie. Daphne can go with Jeremy, and I believe the rest of you have your own cars. Has anyone seen the major?"

Lady Jane spoke up. "He was fishing about on the

other side of the loch, pretending to be an angler. At least it makes a change from pretending to be an officer and a gentleman."

"The rest of you go on to the hotel," said John hurriedly. "I'll go and look for the major."

"I wish you were coming with me," said Jeremy to Alice.

She looked at him in surprise. She had been so obsessed with Mr. Patterson-James that she had never really stopped to think any other man might find her attractive.

As Jeremy moved off with Daphne, Alice studied him covertly. He really was a very attractive man. His voice was pleasant and slightly husky. He did not seem to have to strangle and chew his words as Mr. Patterson-James did. Her heart gave a little lift, and she unconsciously smiled at Jeremy's retreating back.

"No use," said Lady Jane, appearing at Alice's elbow. "He's one of the Somerset Blythes. Quite above your touch, wouldn't you say? Daphne's more his sort."

Alice was consumed by such a wave of bitter hatred that she thought she would suffocate. "Fook off!" she said, in a broad Liverpool accent.

"Attagirl!" remarked Marvin cheerfully.

Lady Jane muttered something. Alice thought

she said, "I'll make you sorry you said that," but she must have been imagining things.

Alice was prepared to find herself cut off from Jeremy for the rest of the day. But when they reached the river Anstey, which broadened out at one part into a large loch, Heather arranged that Jeremy and Alice should take out the rowing boat and fish from there while the rest were distributed up and down the banks several miles apart.

Before she allowed Alice to go out in the boat, Heather gave her a gruelling half-hour lesson in casting. Alice caught her hat, caught the bushes behind, wrapped her leader around the branches of a tree, and then quite suddenly found she had mastered the knack of it.

"Don't keep worrying about all that line racing out behind you," said Heather. "Just concentrate on what you've been told. Now you're ready to go. Jeremy, you've obviously done this before."

"Yes, but very clumsily," said Jeremy.

"Take the boat and row upstream and then drift slowly back down," said Heather. "You may not catch a salmon but you should get some trout."

He rowed them swiftly up the stream while Alice nervously held her rod upright and wondered what on earth she would do if she caught a fish. The day was warm and sunny, and she felt laden down with equipment. Her long green waders were clumsy and heavy. She had a fishing knife in one pocket and mosquito repellent in the other, since clouds of Scottish midges were apt to descend towards dusk.

She had a fishing net hanging from a string around her neck, and from another string a pair of small sharp scissors.

On top of her wool fishing hat, kept back from her face by the thin brim, was a sort of beekeeper mosquito net which could be pulled down over her face if the flies got too bad.

Jeremy rested the oars. "Pooh, it's hot. Let's take some clothes off."

Alice blushed painfully. Of course he meant they should remove some of their outer woollens, but Alice was at an age when everything seemed to sound sexy. She wondered feverishly whether she had a dirty mind.

Thank goodness she had had the foresight to put a thin cotton blouse under her army sweater. Alice took off her hat and then her sweater after unslinging the fishing net and laying it in the bottom of the boat. She kept her scissors around her neck. Heather had been most insistent that they keep a pair of scissors handy for cutting lines and snipping free hooks.

"Well," said Jeremy, "here goes!"

The water was very still and golden in the sun. A hot smell of pine drifted on the air mixed with the smell of wild thyme. Alice felt herself gripped by a desire to catch something—*anything.*

She cast and cast again until her arms ached. And then . . .

"I've got something," she whispered. "It's a salmon. It feels enormous."

Jeremy quickly reeled in his line and picked up his net. "Don't reel in too fast," he said. He picked up the oars and moved the boat gently. Alice's rod began to bend.

"Reel in a bit more," he said.

"Oh, Jeremy," said Alice, pink with excitement, "what am I going to do?"

"Take it easy . . . easy."

Alice could not wait. She reeled in frantically. Suddenly the line came clear, and she jerked it out of the water.

On the end of her hook dangled a long piece of green weed.

"And I thought I had a twenty-pound salmon," mourned Alice. "Do you know, Jeremy, I'm still shaking with excitement. Do you think I'm very primitive, really? I mean, I wouldn't normally hurt a fly, and there I was, ready to kill anything that came up on the end of that hook."

"I don't think you're all that quiet and timid," said Jeremy, casting again. "Only look at the way you put down Lady Jane. I heard all about that."

"I can't believe I did that," said Alice thoughtfully. "I've never used that sort of language to anyone in my life. But it was all so beautiful when we were having lunch, I wanted it to go on forever. Then suddenly she was there, bitching and making trouble. She drops hints, you know. Almost as if she had checked up on us all before she came. She... she told me you belonged to the Somerset Blythes." Alice bit her lip. She had been on the point of telling him the rest.

"She did, did she? Probably one of those women with little else to do with their time. I hope she doesn't make life too hard for the village constable. She probably will complain to his superiors."

"Poor Hamish."

"I think Hamish is well able to take care of himself. And what policeman, do you think, would rush in to take his place? Hardly the spot for an ambitious man."

"What do you do for a living?" asked Alice.

"I'm a barrister."

Alice felt a pang of disappointment. She had been secretly hoping he did something as undistinguished as she did.

"What do you do?" she heard Jeremy asking.

He was wearing a short-sleeved check shirt and a baggy pair of old flannels, but there was a polished air about him, an air of social ease and money. All at once Alice wanted to pretend she was someone different, someone more important.

"I'm chief accountant at Baxter and Berry in the City." She gave a self-conscious laugh. "An odd job for a woman."

"Certainly for someone as young as yourself," said Jeremy. "I didn't think such a fuddy-duddy firm would be so go-ahead."

"You know Baxter and Berry?" queried Alice nervously.

"I know old man Baxter," said Jeremy easily. "He's a friend of my father. I must tease him about his pretty chief accountant."

Alice turned her face away. That's where telling lies got you. Futureless. Now she wouldn't dare even see Jeremy again after this holiday.

"When I was your age, which was probably all of ten years ago," said Jeremy gently, "I told a perfectly smashing-looking girl that I was a jet pilot..."

"Oh, Jeremy," said Alice miserably, "I'm only the chief accountant's secretary."

"Thank you for the compliment." He grinned. "It's a long time since anyone's tried to impress me."

"You're not angry I lied to you?"

"No. Hey, I think you've caught something."

"Probably weed." Alice felt young and free and lighthearted. Mr. Patterson-James's saturnine face swam around in her mind, faded and disappeared like Scotch mist.

She reeled in her line, amused at the tugs, thinking how like a fish floating weed felt.

There was a flash and sparkle in the peaty brown and gold water.

"A trout!" said Jeremy. He held out his net and brought the fish in.

"Too small," he said, shaking his head. "We've got to throw it back."

"Don't hurt it!" cried Alice as he worked the fly free from the fish's mouth.

"No, it's gone back to Mum," he said, throwing it in the water. "What fly were you using?"

"A Kenny's Killer."

He took out his box of fishing flies. "Maybe I'll try one of those."

A companionable silence settled between them. The light began to fade behind the jumbled, twisted crags of the Two Sisters. A little breeze sent ripples lazily fanning out over the loch.

And then out of the heather came the midges, those small Scottish mosquitoes. Alice's face was black with them. She screamed and clawed for her mosquito net while Jeremy rowed quickly for the shore.

"Quick—let's just bundle everything in the car and drive away from the beasts," he said.

Alice scrambled into the bucket seat of something long and low. They shot off down the road, not stopping until they were well clear of the loch. Jeremy handed Alice a towel to wipe her face.

Alice smiled at him gratefully. "What about Daphne? I'd forgotten all about her."

"So had I." Jeremy was shadowed by a stand of trees beside the car. He seemed to be watching her mouth. Alice's heart began to hammer.

"Did...did you buy this car in Scotland?" she asked. "I mean, I thought you and Daphne came up by train."

"We did. My father had been using the car. He knew I was coming up this way and so he left it in Inverness for me to collect."

"You've known Daphne a long time?"

"No. Heather wrote to me to ask me if I would join up with Daphne. She had written to Heather saying she did not like to travel alone."

He suddenly switched on the engine. Alice sat very quietly. Perhaps he might have kissed her if she hadn't kept on and on about stupid Daphne. Daphne was probably back at the hotel changing into some couture number for dinner. Damn Daphne.

"I never thought indecision was one of my failings," said Jeremy, breaking the silence at last. "I don't want to spoil things by going too fast too soon."

Alice was not quite sure if he meant he had wanted to kiss her and had changed his mind. She dared not ask him in case he should be embarrassed and say he was talking about fishing.

But he suddenly took one hand off the wheel and gave her own a quick squeeze.

Alice's heart soared. A huge owl sailed across the winding road. Down below them nestled the village of Lochdubh.

Busy little fishing boats chugged out to sea. The lights of the hotel dining room were reflected in the still waters of the loch. Down into the evening darkness of the valley they sped. Over the old humpbacked bridge which spanned the tumbling waterfalls of the river Anstey. Along the waterfront, past the low white cottages of the village. Out in the loch, a pair of seals rolled and tumbled like two elderly Edwardian gentlemen.

Tears filled Alice's eyes, and she furtively dabbed them away. The beauty of the evening was too much. The beauty of money emanating from the leather smells of the long, low, expensive car and the faint tangy scent of Jeremy's aftershave seduced her senses. She wanted it all. She wanted to keep the evening forever. Scenic beauty, male beauty, money beauty.

A picture of Lady Jane rose large in her mind's eye, blotting out the evening.

If she tries to spoil things for me, I'll kill her, thought Alice passionately.

And being very young and capable of violent mood swings, she then began to worry about what to wear for dinner.

When she entered the dining room an hour later, the rest of the fishing party, except for Lady Jane, Charlie, and the major, was already seated.

To her disappointment, the only available seat was at the other end of the table from Jeremy.

Jeremy was sitting next to Daphne and laughing at something she was saying.

Daphne was wearing a black chiffon cocktail gown slit to the waist so that it afforded the company tantalizing glimpses of two perfect breasts.

Long antique earrings hung in the shadow of the silky bell of her naturally blonde hair. Her usually hard, high-cheek-boned face was softened by eye shadow and pink lipstick.

Jeremy was wearing a well-cut charcoal grey suit, a striped shirt, and a tie with one of those small hard knots. He wore a heavy, pale gold wrist watch.

Alice wished she had worn something different. All her clothes had looked cheap and squalid. At last she had settled for a pale pink cashmere sweater, a tailored shirt, and a row of Woolworth's pearls. She had persuaded herself in the privacy of her bedroom that she looked like a regular member of the county. Now she felt like a London typist trying ineffectually to look like a member of the county. The dining room was very warm.

Amy Roth was wearing a floating sort of chiffony thing in cool blues and greens. It left most of her back bare. At one point, Marvin slid his hand down his wife's back, and Amy wriggled her shoulders and giggled.

Heather was wearing a long gown that looked as if it had been made out of chintz upholstery, but she managed to look like a lady nonetheless, thought Alice gloomily. John Cartwright was cheerful and relaxed, obviously glad that the rigours of the first day were over.

The hotel had contributed several bottles of non-vintage Czechoslovakian champagne, their labels discreetly hidden by white napkins.

The food was delicious—poached salmon with a good hollandaise sauce. Everyone began to relax and become slightly tipsy.

Emboldened by the wine, Alice decided to forget

about Jeremy and talk to the Roths. Marvin, it transpired, was a New Yorker born and bred, but Amy hailed from Augusta, Georgia. Marvin was her third husband, she told Alice, very much in the way a woman would describe an expensive gown that had been a good buy.

Marvin was quiet and polite and very deferential to his wife, the way Alice imagined American men should be. She began to wonder if she had really heard him shouting earlier in the day, but the Roths did seem to be the only Americans in the hotel.

The party grew noisier and jollier.

And then Major Peter Frame came stumbling in. His eyes were staring, and his hands were trembling. He clutched on to a chair back and looked wildly around the group.

"Where is that bitch?" he grated.

"If you mean Lady Jane," said Heather, "I really don't know. What on earth is the matter?"

"I'll tell you," said the major with frightening intensity. "I went back up to the Marag this evening, just above the falls. And I got one. A fifteen-pounder on the end of my line. It was a long battle, and I was resting my fish and having a smoke when she comes blundering along like an ox. 'Can I get past?' she says. 'Your line's blocking the path.' 'I've got a big 'un on the end of that line,' I says. 'Don't be silly,' says she. 'I can't wait here all night. It's probably a rock,' and before I could guess what she meant to do she whipped out her scissors *and cut my line*. She cut my line, the bloody bitch. The great, fat, stinking *cow*.

"I'll murder her. I'll kill that horrible woman. Kill! Kill! Kill!"

The major's voice had risen to a scream. Shocked silence fell on the dining room.

And into the middle of the silence sailed Lady Jane.

She was wearing a pink chiffon evening gown with a great many bows and tucks and flounces; the type of evening gown favoured by the Queen Mother, Barbara Cartland, and Danny La Rue.

"Well, we're all very glum," she said, amused eyes glancing around the stricken group. "Now, what can I do to brighten up the party?"

Day Two

Then as the earth's inner, narrow crooked lanes
Do purge salt waters' fretful tears away

—John Donne

Alice fumbled with a sleepy hand to silence the buzzing of her travel alarm and stretched and yawned. Her room was bathed in a grey light. She had forgotten to close the curtains before going to bed. Fat, greasy raindrops trickled down the window.

Somehow the horrible first dinner had miraculously turned out all right. Lady Jane had carried all before her. Before the major had had time to round on her, Lady Jane had apologized with such an overwhelming blast of sincerity and charm, with such subtle underlying appeals to his status as an officer and gentleman, that the major's angry colour had subsided, and, after that, people had begun to enjoy themselves. It was Lady Jane who had suggested that they should all get together in the lounge after dinner and help each other tie their leaders. It was Lady Jane who had kept the party laughing with a flow of faintly malicious anecdotes.

Alice remembered Jeremy's well-manicured hands brushing against her own and the smell of his after-shave as he had bent his head close to hers to help her tie knots. He had seemed to lose interest in Daphne.

There was to be another lecture that morning before they went out fishing for the day. Alice got out of bed and went to the window and looked out. She could not even see the harbour. A thick mist blanketed everything and the rain thudded steadily down. Perhaps she would be lucky and would be teamed up with Jeremy again. Alice closed her eyes, imagining them both eating their packed lunches in the leather-smelling warmth of Jeremy's car with the steamed-up windows blocking out the rest of the world.

After a hasty shower, she took out her pink plastic rollers and tried to comb her hair into a more sophisticated style, but it fluffed out as usual.

To her dismay, they were not all to be seated at the same table for breakfast, and she was ushered to a table where the major was already eating sausages. Jeremy was with Daphne and Lady Jane at the other end of the dining room.

The major glanced at Alice and then rustled open a copy of *The Times*—last Friday's—and began to study the social column.

"Wet, isn't it?" volunteered Alice brightly, but the major only grunted in reply.

Probably doesn't think I'm worth talking to, thought Alice gloomily.

She rose and helped herself to cereal and rolls and juice, which were placed on a table in the centre of the room, and then shyly ordered the Fisherman's Breakfast from a massive waitress who was built like a Highland cow.

When the breakfast arrived, she poked at it tentatively with a fork. Bacon, eggs, and sausage, she recognized, but the rest seemed odd and strange.

"What are these?" she asked the major. He did not reply so she repeated her question in a rather shrill voice.

"Haggis and black pudding and a potato scone," said the major. "Very good. Scotch stuff, you know. Introduced to the stuff when I was first in the Highlands on military training."

"Were you in the SAS?" asked Alice.

"No." The major smiled indulgently. "They hadn't been formed in my day. We called ourselves something else."

"Oh, what was that?"

"Mustn't say. Hush-hush stuff, you know."

"Oh." Alice was impressed.

"Of course I was in the regular army for most of the big show."

"Which was . . . ?"

"World War Two. Can still remember leading my men up the Normandy beaches. Yanks had taken the easy bits and left us with the cliffs. 'Don't worry, chaps,' I said. 'We'll take Jerry this time.' They believed me, bless their hearts. Would have died for me. 'Straordinary loyalty. Quite touching, 's matter of fact."

Alice wished her mum could see her now. "Quite one of the old school," Mum would say.

"Tell me more," urged Alice, eyes glowing.

"Well," said the major happily. "There was a time . . ."

His voice faded away as a bulky shadow fell across the table. Alice looked up. Lady Jane's pale eyes surveyed the major with amusement. "Telling Miss Wilson all your tales of derring-do? All those pitched battles around the tea tent on Salisbury Plain?"

Now what could there be in those remarks to make the major sweat? Alice looked from one to the other. Lady Jane nodded her head and gave a little smile before walking away.

The major looked after her, mumbled something, and went off mopping his forehead with his handkerchief.

Charlie Baxter, the Roths, and all the rest were already in the lounge. A cheerful fire was blazing on the hearth. The heavyset waitress lumbered in and threw a pile of old tea leaves, cabbage stalks, and old rolls on the fire, which subsided into a depressing, smoking mess.

Heather examined all their leaders and tugged at the knots. Several gave way. "I wish you wouldn't say you can tie these things when you obviously can't," said Lady Jane to the major.

"You are supposed to tie them yourselves," pointed out Heather.

"Like a bloody schoolroom," muttered Lady Jane. "Oh, here's that wretched man again."

Constable Macbeth lounged in, water dripping from his black cape. He removed it and squatted down by the fire, raking aside the sodden lumps of congealed goo and putting on fresh coal and sticks. Then, to Alice's amusement, he lay down on his stomach and began to blow furiously until the flames started leaping up the chimney.

"This hotel has central heating, hasn't it?" Amy Roth shivered. "Why doesn't someone turn it on?"

"Now I want you all to try to tie your leaders

properly this time," came Heather's voice. Everyone groaned and began to wrestle with the thin, slippery nylon.

Constable Macbeth had ambled over to an armchair by the window. Suddenly Alice saw him stiffen. It was almost as if he had pointed like a dog. He got to his feet, his tall, thin frame silhouetted against the greyness of the day.

Overcome by curiosity, Alice rose quietly and walked to the window. Whatever, or whoever, Constable Macbeth was looking at was absorbing his whole attention.

Alice looked out.

A slim, blonde girl was getting out of a Land Rover. She had a yellow oilskin coat and shooting breeches and green Wellington boots. Her beautiful face was a calm, well-bred oval. She was struggling to lift a heavy wicker basket out of the Land Rover.

The policeman turned around so quickly he nearly fell over Alice. He seized his cape and darted from the room and reappeared a moment later below the window. He said something to the girl, who laughed up at him. He leaned across her and wrested the basket from the Land Rover. The girl locked the car, and then they walked away, the constable carrying the basket.

I wonder who she is, thought Alice. Rich-looking

with that cold sort of damn-you stare. Not a hope there, Lady Jane would no doubt say.

"This goddamn thing has a life of its own," came Marvin Roth's voice.

"What we need," said Lady Jane, "is some useful slave labour. Some *sweated* labour, wouldn't you say, Mr Roth?"

"Watch that mouth of yours, lady," grated Marvin Roth.

There was a shocked silence. Oh dear, thought Heather, I should never have tried to cope with them alone. That dreadful woman. She keeps saying things which sound innocuous to me but which seem terribly barbed to the person they're directed against. She's got that mottled red about the neck which usually means high blood pressure. I wish she would drop dead.

"And now," said Heather out loud, amazed to hear how shaky her own voice sounded, "I will pass round some pieces of string and teach you how to tie a figure of eight."

To Heather's relief, her husband came into the room. "We're running a bit late," he said. "Better get them started. We'll issue them with rods again, that is, the ones who want to rent stuff—I think only the major has brought his own—and then we'll get them off to the Upper Alsh and Loch Alsh."

Alice pulled on her waders in her room and checked she had everything tucked away in the pockets of her green fowling coat—scissors, a needle (for poking out the eyes of flies—artificial ones, she had been glad to find out—and for undoing knots), and a penknife. She placed her fishing hat on her head and made her way back downstairs, hoping the other guests thought she was a seasoned fisherwoman.

In the car park, John was passing out maps, explaining that Loch Alsh was some distance away. Water dripped from his hat on to his nose. Rain thudded down on the car park. "At least it will keep the flies away," he said. "Now, let me see—Jeremy, you'll take Daphne." Alice had a sinking feeling in her stomach as John went on to say she was to come along with himself and Heather and young Charlie Baxter. Alice felt Lady Jane's eyes on her face and angrily jerked her already sodden hat down on her forehead.

The journey seemed endless. The mountains were blotted out by the mist. The windscreen wipers clicked monotonously back and forth. Alice looked at Charlie. He was hunched in the far corner. Alice did not know what one talked to children about. "Enjoying yourself?" she asked at last.

The child's hard, assessing gaze was fixed on

her face. "No," he said at last. "I hate that ugly fat woman. She's cruel and mean and evil. Why doesn't she die? Lots of people die in the Highlands. They get lost and starve and die of exposure. They fall off cliffs. Why can't something happen to *her*?"

"Now, now," said Alice reprovingly. "Mustn't talk like that."

There was a long silence, then, "You're very silly, you know," said the child in a conversational tone of voice.

Alice coloured up. "Don't be impertinent."

"*You* were being impertinent," said the maddening Charlie. "Anyway, you hate her just as much as I do."

"If you mean Lady Jane, she *is* very trying," said Heather over one plump shoulder. "But her faults seem worse because we're such a small group. You wouldn't notice her much in a crowd."

"*I* would," said Charlie, putting an effective end to that bit of conversation.

Alice began to feel carsick. The big estate car swayed on the slick macadam surface of the road and cruised up and down over the many rises and bumps.

At last the car veered sharply left and lurched even more over a dirt track where clumps of heather scraped the side of the car.

When Alice was just about ready to scream that she was about to be sick, they lurched to a halt.

She climbed out, feeling stiff and cold.

A rain-pocked loch stretched out in front of her and vanished into the mist. All was still and silent except for the constant drumming of the rain. Heather and John began to unload the rods as the others drove up.

"Now, who wants to row the boat?"

"Me!" cried Charlie, showing rare animation.

"Then you can be my ghillie," said Lady Jane, a ghillie being a Highland servant. "Too many bushes around here. I'd be better in the middle of the loch."

"With a stone around your fat neck," muttered Amy Roth. She caught Alice staring at her and blushed like a schoolgirl. "She's such a lady," thought Alice, amused. "I bet she feels like fainting any time she says 'damn'."

Heather hesitated. Charlie was looking horrified at the idea of rowing Lady Jane. On the other hand, Charlie seemed to be the one member of the party that Lady Jane had so far not managed to intimidate. And he could be rescued after an hour.

"Very well," said Heather. "The Roths and the major can go with John further up the loch and fish the river. We should get good brown trout or small salmon so you will only need light rods."

"What about me?" asked Alice.

"You come with me and I'll start you off," said Heather. "Jeremy, you go along to the left and Daphne to the right. Keep moving now. We'll only fish for a little bit and then we'll meet back here in two hours' time."

Alice kept looking hopefully in Jeremy's direction while they assembled their rods. Daphne had caught her fly in her jacket, and Jeremy was laughing and joking as he wiggled it free for her.

Alice shivered. The rain had found its way inside her collar.

"Come along," said Heather. "No, don't carry your rod like that, Alice. You'll either spear someone or get it caught in a bush."

Jeremy waded off into the loch, and Alice watched him go until he was swallowed up in the mist. Lady Jane's petulant voice sounded over the water, "Can't you row a little harder?" Poor Charlie.

Alice waded along the shallows after Heather. "Just here, I think," said Heather. "Try casting here."

Wet and miserable, Alice jerked her rod back and caught the bush behind her. "No, like this," said Heather patiently, after she had extricated Alice's hook. She took Alice's arm in a firm grasp and cast the fly so neatly that it landed on the water without a ripple. "Good," murmured Heather. "Now again. And again."

Alice's arm began to ache. She cursed and stumbled and slipped on the slippery boulders in the water beneath her feet. "I'll try a little bit further on," said Heather placidly. "You're doing just grand. Remember to stop the rod at the twelve o'clock position. The loch's quite shallow for a good bit, so if you move slowly out from the shore, you might get a bite and then you don't have the risk of getting your hook caught in the bushes."

Why don't I just say I'll never learn how to fish and I don't care, thought Alice wretchedly. Jeremy's not interested in me. I don't belong here. But somehow she found herself wading slowly out into the loch, casting as she went.

Then the line went taut.

Alice's heart leapt into her mouth.

It was probably a rock or a bit of weed. She began to reel in, feeling with growing excitement the tugs and shivers on the line. A trout leapt in the air at the end of the line and dived.

"Help!" screamed Alice, red with excitement. Would Heather never come? What if she lost it? She could not *bear* to lose it. Seized with a fever almost as old as the hills around her, Alice reeled in her line.

"That's it," said Heather quietly, appearing suddenly at Alice's side. "Get your net ready."

"Net. Yes, net," said Alice, scrabbling wildly about and dropping her rod in the water. Heather bent down and seized the rod.

"Get the net ready," said Heather again. Alice wanted to snatch the rod back but was afraid of losing the fish. Forward it came, turning and glistening in the water. Alice scooped the net under it and lifted it up, watching the fish with a mixture of exultation and pity.

"Quite a big one," said Heather. "Three pounds, I should think. It'll make a good breakfast." She led the way to the shore after removing the hook from the trout's mouth.

"Can't you kill it?" asked Alice, looking at the panting, struggling fish. "Oh yes," said Heather, slowly picking up a rock. All her movements were slow and sure. "We'll just put it out of its misery."

How abhorrent the idea of killing things seemed in London, thought Alice, and how natural it seemed in this savage landscape. Heather slid the trout into a plastic bag. "Put that in your fishing bag," she said to Alice. "It's about time for lunch. I think I hear the others returning."

Alice was the only one who had caught anything and received lavish praise from everyone but

Lady Jane and Charlie Baxter. The child looked exhausted, and Heather was fussing over him, helping him into the front seat of the car and pouring him hot tea.

"You're a marvel, Alice," said Jeremy. "Did you really catch that brute all by yourself?"

"Yes, did you *really*?" asked Lady Jane.

Alice hesitated only for a moment. Heather was a little bit away, hopefully out of earshot. "Yes," said Alice loudly. "Yes, I did."

"I'd better keep close to you this afternoon," grinned Jeremy. "Seems you have all the luck."

Alice's pleasure was a little dimmed by, first, the lie she had told, which she was now sure Heather had overheard, and, second, by the fact that Jeremy and Daphne were to share a cozy lunch in his car while she herself was relegated to the back of the Cartwrights' estate car.

Lunch tasted rather nasty. Great slabs of pâté, cold and heavy, and dry yellow cake and boiled eggs. But the fishing fever had Alice in its grip, and she could hardly wait to try her luck again. Somehow, Alice felt, if she managed to catch another fish all on her own then the lie would be forgiven by the gods above. For the first few moments after they climbed from the cars again, it looked as if the day's fishing might have to be cancelled. A wind had risen and was driving great buffets of rain into their faces.

"It said on the forecast this morning it might dry up later," yelled John above the noise of the rising wind. "I say we ought to give it another half-hour."

Everyone agreed, since no one wanted to return home without a fish. If Alice could catch one, then anyone could, was the general opinion.

"I'm all right now," Charlie said, after Heather had towelled his curls dry. "It was that woman. Row here. Row there. And then she said...she said... never mind."

"Slide along behind the wheel, Charlie," said Heather firmly. "I really think you ought to tell me what Lady Jane said to upset you."

But Charlie would only shake his drying curls and look stubborn.

Heather was determined to have a word with her husband about Lady Jane as soon as possible. But the roar of an engine told her that John was already setting out with the major for the upper beats of the river.

"Would you like me to run you back to the hotel?" she asked the boy.

He shook his head. "As long as I can fish alone," he said. "I'll wait with the rest and see if the weather lifts."

Alice was oblivious to the slashing rain as she waded out into the loch again with Jeremy at her side, deaf to the sounds of altercation from the shore as Heather told Lady Jane firmly that she was to leave Charlie alone and drive to the upper beats to join the major, the Roths, and John.

"Brrrr, it's cold," said Jeremy. "Where did you catch your trout?"

"Just here," said Alice. "I'll show you." She cast wildly and heard the fly plop in the water behind her, then clumsily whipped the line forward. "I'm tired," she said defiantly, "and my arm aches. That's why I can't do it right."

"Look, it's like this," said Jeremy. "Keep your legs apart"—Alice blushed—"with the left foot slightly forward. Bring the rod smartly up towards your shoulder using the forearm and hold your upper arms close to your body. When you make the back flick, the line should stream out straight behind, and when you feel a tug at the top of the line, you'll know the back cast is completed, and then bring it into the forward cast."

Alice's line cracked like a lion tamer's whip. "Are you sure you caught that fish yourself?" laughed Jeremy.

"Of course I did," said Alice with the steady, out-raged gaze of the liar.

"I'll try further down," said Jeremy, beginning to wade away. "I wonder if Daphne's had any luck."

Damn Daphne, thought Alice savagely. All her elation had fled, leaving her alone in the middle of a howling wilderness of wind and rain.

She simply *had* to get Jeremy back.

Remembering everything she had been taught, she balanced herself on the slippery pebbles under the water and cast carefully and neatly towards Jeremy's retreating back.

"Caught 'im," thought Alice. Aloud, she called, "Sorry, Jeremy darling. I'm afraid I've hooked *you*." Now, in the romances that Alice read, Jeremy should have said something like, "You caught me a long time ago," and then walked slowly towards her and taken her in his powerful arms.

What he did say in fact was, "Silly bitch. There's the whole loch to fish from. Come here and help me get this hook out."

Blushing and stumbling, Alice edged miserably towards him. The hook was embedded in the back of his jacket. She twisted and pulled and finally it came free with a ripping sound.

Jeremy twisted an anguished face over his shoulder. "Now look what you've done. Look, just keep well clear of me." He waded off into the driving rain.

Tears of humiliation mixed with the rainwater on Alice's face. She felt hurt and lost and alone. Her face ached with trying to maintain a posh accent. Jeremy would never have behaved like that with someone of his own class.

She decided to turn about, give up, and go back and shelter in the car until this horrible day's fishing was all over.

Alice stumbled towards the shore. Suddenly the water turned gold. Sparkling gold with red light dancing in the peaty ripples. She turned and looked towards the west. Blue sky was spreading rapidly over the heavens. Mountains stood up, sharp and prehistoric with their twisted, deformed shapes. Heather blazed in great, glorious clumps, and the sun beat down on Alice's sopping hat.

"Alice! Alice!" Jeremy was churning towards her through the water, holding up a fairly small trout.

"Marvellous girl." He beamed. "Knew you would bring me luck." He threw his arms around her, slapping her on the back of the head with his dead trout as he did so.

Transported from hell to heaven, Alice smiled back. "Come along," said Jeremy. "I've got a flask of brandy in the car. Let's take a break and celebrate."

While Jeremy got his flask, Alice took off her hat and her wet coat and put them both on the bushes to dry. Jeremy sat down on a rock beside her and handed her the flask and she choked over an enormous gulp of brandy.

The liqueur shot down to her stomach and up to her brain. She felt dizzy with happiness. They had had their first quarrel, she thought dreamily. How they would laugh about it after they were married!

Elated with brandy and sunshine, they cheerfully agreed to return to the loch and try their luck again. And Alice did try. Very hard. If only she could catch a fish all by herself then she could be easy in her conscience.

But at four in the afternoon, Heather appeared to call them to the cars. They were to return to the hotel for another fishing lecture.

Even Alice felt sulkily that it was all too much like being back at school. Why waste a perfectly good afternoon sitting indoors in a stuffy hotel lounge?

But none of them had quite realized how tired they were until John Cartwright began his lecture on fly tying. Despite the heat from the sun pouring in the long windows, a log fire was burning, its flames bleached pale by the sunlight. A bluebottle buzzed against the windows.

While Heather's nimble fingers demonstrated the art of fly tying, John discoursed on the merits of wet and dry flies. Names like Tup's Indispensable, Little Claret, Wickman's Fancy, Black Pennell and Cardinal floated like dust motes on the hot, somnolent air. "Sound like racehorses," said Jeremy sleepily.

Alice felt her eyes beginning to close. The major was asleep, twitching in his armchair like an old dog; the Roths were leaning together, joined by fatigue into a fireside picture of a happily married couple. Lady Jane had her eyes half closed, like a basking lizard; and Daphne Gore was painting her nails vermillion.

Suddenly Alice jerked her eyes open. There was a feeling of fear in the room, fear mixed with malice.

While John droned on, Heather had stopped her demonstration to flip through the post. She was sitting very still, holding an airmail letter in her plump hands. She raised her eyes and looked at Lady Jane. Lady Jane raised her heavy lids and smiled. It was not a nice smile.

Heather's face had gone putty-coloured. She put a hand on her husband's sleeve and passed him the letter. He glanced at it and then began to read it closely, his lips folded into a grim line.

"Class dismissed," he said at last, putting down the letter and assuming a rather ghastly air of levity.

"What was all that about?" murmured Jeremy to

Alice. "And why do I feel it has something to do with Lady Jane?"

"Care for a drink before dinner, Jeremy?" came Daphne's cool voice.

"Are you paying?" asked Jeremy, his face crinkling up in a smile.

"What's this? Men's lib?" Daphne slid her arm into his and they left the lounge together. Alice stood stock still, biting her lip.

"I told you you were wasting your time." Lady Jane's large bulk hove up on Alice's port side.

Fury like bile nearly choked Alice. "You are a horrible, unpleasant woman," she grated.

This seemed to increase Lady Jane's good humour. "Now, now," she purred. "Little girls in glass houses shouldn't throw stones. And I *do* trust our stone-throwing days are over."

Alice gazed at her in terror. She *knew*. She would tell Jeremy. She would tell *everybody*.

She turned and ran and did not stop running until she reached her room. She threw herself face down on the bed and cried and cried until she could cry no more. And then she became conscious of all that barbaric wilderness of Highland moor and mountain outside. Accidents happened. Anything could happen. Alice pictured Lady Jane's heavy body plummeting down into a salmon pool, her fat face lifeless, turned upwards in the brown, peaty water. Abruptly, she fell asleep.

When she awoke, she thought it was still early because of the daylight outside, forgetting about the long light of a northern Scottish summer.

Then she saw it was ten o'clock. With a gasp, she hurtled from the bed and washed and changed. But when she went down to the dining room, it was to find that dinner was over and she had to put up with sandwiches served in the bar. Everyone seemed to have gone to bed. The barman informed her that the fat FEB had gone out walking and perhaps the other was with her—that Lady Whatsername. Alice asked curiously what a FEB was but the bartender said hurriedly he "shouldnae hae said that" and polished glasses furiously.

CHARLIE BAXTER THREW leaves into the river Anstey from the humpbacked bridge and watched them being churned into the boiling water and then tossed up again on their turbulent road to the sea. His aunt, Mrs. Pargeter, thought he was safely in bed, but he had put on his clothes and climbed out of the window. His mother had written to say she would be arriving at the end of the week. Charlie looked forward to her visit and dreaded it at the same time. He still could not quite believe he would never see his father again. Mother had won custody of him in a violent divorce case and talked endlessly about defying the law and keeping Charlie away from his father for life. Charlie felt miserably that it was somehow all his fault; that if he had been a better child then his parents might have stayed together. He turned from the bridge and headed towards the hotel.

The sky and sea were pale grey, setting off the black twisted shapes of the mountains crouched behind the village.

Charlie walked along the harbour, watching the men getting ready for their night's fishing. He was debating asking one of them if he could go along and was just rejecting the idea as hopeless—for surely they would demand permission from his aunt—when a soft voice said behind him, "Isn't it time you were in bed, young man?"

Charlie glanced up. The tall figure of Constable Macbeth loomed up in the dusk. "I was just going home," muttered Charlie.

"Well, I'll just take a bit of a walk with you. It's a grand night."

"As a matter of fact, my aunt doesn't know I'm out," said Charlie.

"Then we would not want to be upsetting Mrs. Pargeter," said Hamish equably. "But we'll take a wee dauner along the front."

As Hamish Macbeth was turning away, a voice sounded from an open window of the hotel, "Throw the damn thing away. It's like poison." Mrs Cartwright, thought Charlie. Then came John Cartwright's voice, "Oh, very well. But you're worrying overmuch. I'll throw this in the loch and then we can maybe get a night's sleep."

A crumpled piece of blue paper sailed past Charlie's head and landed on the oily stones of the beach. The tide was out.

Charlie picked it up. It was a crumpled airmail. "You shouldn't look at other people's correspondence," said Hamish Macbeth severely, "even though they may have chucked it away."

"I wasn't going to read it. It's got a lovely stamp. Austrian."

They passed the Roths, who were walking some distance apart. Marvin's face was flushed and Amy's mouth was turned down at the corners. "Hi!" said Marvin, forcing a smile.

"It's a grand night," remarked the policeman. The American couple went on their way, and Charlie hurriedly thrust the airmail into his pocket.

When they reached his aunt's house, Charlie said shyly, "Do you mind leaving me here? I know how to get in without waking her."

Hamish Macbeth nodded, but waited at the garden

gate until the boy disappeared around the side of the house.

Then he made his way home to his own house where his dog, Towser, gave him a slavering welcome. Hamish absentmindedly stroked the animal's rough coat. There was something about this particular fishing class that was making him uneasy.

Day Three

*Thy tongue imagineth wickedness: and with lies
thou cuttest like a sharp razor.*

—The Psalms

Alice had reasoned herself into an optimistic frame
of mind, although anxiety had first roused her at six
in the morning. She had dressed and had taken herself out on a walk up the hill behind the hotel.

A light, gauzy mist lay on everything, pearl-
ing the long grass and wild thyme, lying on the
rippling silk of the loch, and drifting around the
gnarled trunks of old twisted pines, last remnants of
the Caledonian forest. Harebells shivered as Alice
moved slowly through the grass, and a squirrel
looked at her curiously before darting up a tree.

Alice sat on a rock and talked severely to herself. The youthful peccadillo that had landed her
briefly in the juvenile court was something buried

in the mists of time. Why, her mother's neighbours in Liverpool hardly remembered it! It was certainly something that Lady Jane could *not* know about. It had appeared in the local paper, circulation eight thousand, in a little paragraph at the bottom of page two. At the time, it had seemed as if the eyes and the ears of the world's press had been on her when she had read that little paragraph. But now she was older and wiser and knew that she had been of no interest whatsoever to the media. That was the hell of being so hypersensitive. You began to think people meant all sorts of things because of their lightest remarks. Who was Lady Jane anyway? Just some silly, bitchy, discontented housewife. Jeremy had said she had been married to Lord John Winters, a choleric backbencher in Wilson's government, who had died of a heart attack only two months after he had received his peerage for nameless services.

Then there was Daphne Gore. Alice envied Daphne's obvious money and cool poise. Lady Jane hadn't been able to get at her. But she, Alice, must not let her own silly snobbery stand in the way of luring Jeremy away from Daphne. Come to think of it, Lady Jane had not riled Jeremy either. Perhaps that was what money and a public school gave you—armour plating.

*   *   *

JOHN CARTWRIGHT AWOKE with an unaccustomed feeling of dread. Certainly, he was used to enduring a bit of stage fright before the beginning of each new fishing class, but that soon disappeared, leaving him with only the heady pleasure of being paid for communicating to others his hobby and his passion...fishing.

Now Lady Jane loomed like a fat thundercloud on the horizon.

Perhaps he was taking the whole thing too seriously. But neither he nor Heather had really performed their duties very well this week. Usually, they meticulously took their class through more intensive instruction on casting, leader tying, fly tying and the habits of the wily salmon. But so far both of them had been only too glad to get their charges out on the water, as if spreading them as far apart as possible could diffuse the threatening atmosphere. There was nothing they could do—legally—to protect themselves from Lady Jane. There were two alternatives. They could pray—or they could murder Lady Jane. But John did not believe in God, and he shrank from the idea of violence. Lady Jane had been charming at dinner last night and seemed to be enjoying herself. Perhaps he could appeal to her better nature...if she had one.

The mist was burning off the loch when the class assembled in the lounge. It promised to be a scorching day. Alice was wearing a blue-and-white gingham blouse with a pair of brief white cotton shorts that showed her long, slim legs to advantage. She was wearing a cheap, oversweet perfume that delighted Jeremy's nostrils. Women who wore cheap scent always seemed so much more approachable, conjuring up memories of tumbled flannel sheets in bedsitting rooms. She was concentrating on practising to tie knots, her fine, fluffy brown hair falling over her forehead. He went to sit beside her on the sofa, edging close to her so that his thigh touched her bare legs. Alice flushed, and her hands trembled a little. "You look delicious this morning," murmured Jeremy and put a hand lightly on her knee. Alice realized, all in that delightful moment, that her knees could blush.

"I am so glad to meet a young man who actually pursues single girls," commented Lady Jane to the world at large. "I'm one of those old-fashioned women who believe adultery to be a sin, the next worst thing to seducing servants."

This remark, which sounded like something from *Upstairs Downstairs*, went largely unnoticed, but it had an odd effect on both Jeremy and Daphne Gore. Jeremy slowly removed his hand from Alice's knee and sat very still. Daphne dropped her coffee cup and swore. "No good comes of it," pursued Lady Jane. "I've known girls run off and make fools of themselves with Spanish waiters and young men who seduce married barmaids. Disgusting!"

There was a long silence. Daphne's distress was all too evident, and Jeremy looked sick.

"Of course," came Constable Macbeth's soft Highland voice, "some of us are protected from the sins of the flesh by our very age and appearance. Would not you say so, Lady Jane?"

"Are you trying to insult me, Officer?"

"Not I. I would be in the way of thinking that it would be an almost impossible thing to do."

Lady Jane's massive bosom swelled under the thin puce silk of her blouse. She's like the Hulk, thought Alice. Any moment now she's going to turn green and explode.

"Were I not aware of the impoverished circumstances of your family," said Lady Jane, "I would stop you from scrounging coffee. Six little brothers and sisters to support, eh? And your aged parents in Ross and Cromarty? So improvident to have children when one is middle-aged. They can turn out retarded, you know."

"Better they turn out retarded—although they're not—than grow up into a silly, fat, middle-aged, barren bitch like yourself," said Hamish with a sweet smile.

"You will suffer for this," howled Lady Jane. "Don't you know who I am? Don't you know the power I have?"

"No," said Amy Roth flatly. "We don't."

Lady Jane opened and shut her mouth like a landed trout.

"That's right, honey," said Marvin Roth. "You can huff and you can puff, but you ain't gonna blow any houses down here. You can make other folks' lives a misery with your snide remarks, but I'm a New Yorker, born and bred, and Amy here's a Blanchard of the Augusta, Georgia, Blanchards and you won't find a tougher combination than that."

A strange change came over Lady Jane. One minute she looked about to suffer the same fate as her late husband; the next, her angry colour had died and she looked around lovingly at Amy.

"Dear me," she said sweetly, "a Blanchard born and bred?"

"Yes, ma'am," said Marvin Roth proudly. "Amy's *old* money, just like the Rockefellers."

"Please!" called John Cartwright. "Let me begin or we'll never get the day started."

They shuffled their chairs into a semicircle. Heather unrolled a screen and then started setting up a small projector. "Lantern slides," groaned Lady Jane.

A tic appeared in John's left cheek, but he gamely went on with his lecture, showing slides of what salmon looked like when they headed up river from the sea, when they were spawning, and when they were returning to the sea.

"Our prices at this school are very reasonable," said John. "*Very* reasonable," he repeated firmly after Lady Jane snorted. "The better-class salmon beats are all strictly preserved and can only usually be fished at enormous cost. Salmon are fly-caught, particularly the ones of small size, on ordinary reservoir-strength trout rods. Regular salmon anglers, however, also include in their tackle longer rods, some designed for two-handed casting, larger reels, heavier lines, stouter leaders, and flies much bigger on average than those used for trout."

"If we had a decent government in power," interrupted Lady Jane, "instead of that Thatcher woman's dictatorship, then *everyone* would be able to fish for salmon, even the common people."

John sighed and signalled to Heather to pack up the projector. He and Heather loved the Sutherland countryside, and he usually ended his talk by showing beautiful colour slides of rivers and mountains and lochs. But he felt beauty would be wasted

on the present gathering. "We will fish the Upper
Sutherland today. Heather will pass around maps.
The pools on the upper river are small, easy to fish,
closely grouped together and within easy distance
of the road. During the summer, the fish cannot get
over the Sutherland falls and so that's why they concentrate in the upper beats. On your map, you will
see the Slow Pool marked. This is a very good holding pool, but it is particularly good in high water
when it is best fished from the right bank. Heather
and I will take Alice and Charlie and the rest of you
can follow as before."

The day was gloriously hot, and even Charlie
Baxter lost his customary reserve and whistled
cheerfully as the large estate car swung around the
hairpin bends of the Highland roads. At one point
a military plane roared overhead, flying so low the
noise of its jets was deafening. "A Jaguar!" said
Charlie.

John fiddled with the knobs of the car radio. A
blast of Gaelic keening split the air. He tried again.
Gaelic. "Isn't there anything in English?" asked
Alice, feeling the more cut off from civilization by
the sound of that incomprehensible tongue coming
from the radio. "She's got a ticket to ride" roared the
Beatles, and everyone laughed and joined in. There
was something about the scorching sun and clear

air that reduced the likes of Lady Jane to a dot on the horizon. Alice could now well understand why people once thought the night hideous with evil creatures.

Alice was only sorry the estate car was big enough to take their rods lying down flat in the back. It would have been jolly to have them poking upright out of the open window, advertising to the world at large that she was a professional fisher of salmon.

They parked in a disused quarry and climbed out to meet the others. Lady Jane was wearing a Greek fisherman's hat that gave her fleshy face with its curved beak of a nose an oddly hermaphroditic appearance.

John spread out the map on the bonnet of the car and sorted them out into pairs. Daphne and Lady Jane were to fish the Calm Pool, a good holding pool, and were told that the streamy water at the top was best. The major and Jeremy were to try their chances at the Slow Pool; the Roths at the Silver Bank; and Alice and Charlie at the Sheiling. Heather would go with Alice and Charlie and John with the major and Jeremy.

Alice fished diligently until Heather announced they should break for lunch. Fishing fever had her in its grip and she had not thought of Jeremy once.

At lunch it transpired that Lady Jane and the major were missing. Jeremy said the local ghillie from Lochdubh had taken him aside and begun talking to him, and the major had packed up and left with him. Daphne said crossly that Lady Jane had thrashed her line about the water enough to scare away a whale and then had mercifully disappeared.

The absence of Lady Jane acted on the spirits of the party like champagne. Heather had augmented the hotel lunch with homemade sausage rolls, potato scones, and fruit bread covered in lashings of butter and strawberry jam. Alice was dreamily happy to see that Daphne's skin was turning an ugly red in the sun while her own was turning to pale gold. A little breeze fanned their hot cheeks and Jeremy made Alice's day perfect by opting to fish with her for the rest of the afternoon.

After some time, Jeremy suggested they should take a rest. Alice lay back on the springy heather by the water's edge and stared dreamily up into the blue sky.

"What do you think of Lady Jane?" asked Jeremy abruptly. Alice propped herself up on one elbow. "I dunno," she said cautiously. "I think she's learned the knack of fishing of a different sort. I think she knows everyone's got some sort of skeleton in the cupboard and she throws out remarks at random and watches until she sees she's caught someone. Like with you and Daphne this morning. Whatever she meant by that servant and Spanish waiter remark, it upset you and Daphne no end."

"Nonsense," said Jeremy quickly. "I was upset for Daphne's sake. I could see the remark had got home." But you were upset *before*, thought Alice. "I think the woman's plain mad. All that talk about her having power is pure rot. She's nothing but the widow of some obscure Labour peer. She's not even good class. I phoned my father about her the other night. He says she's the daughter of old Marie Phipps, who was secretary to and mistress of Lord Chalcont, and Marie forced his lordship into sending Jane to a finishing school in Switzerland. There never was a Mr. Phipps, you know."

"You mean, she's *illegitimate*," gasped Alice. "How splendid. I'd like to throw that in her face."

"Don't, for God's sake," said Jeremy harshly. "She'd bite back like a viper."

"But you said she's got no power."

"Hasn't any power," corrected Jeremy automatically, and Alice hated him for that brief moment. "It's just that I'm thinking of standing for Parliament and I'm very careful about avoiding enemies."

"You'd be marvellous," breathed Alice. Why, he

could be Prime Minister! Maggie Thatcher couldn't live forever.

"You're a funny, intense little thing," said Jeremy. He leaned forward and kissed her on the lips, a firm but schoolboyish embrace. "Now, let's go fish." He grinned.

Alice waded dizzily into the Sheiling, her legs trembling, a sick feeling of excitement churning in her stomach. The future Prime Minister of Britain had just kissed her! "No comment," she said to the clamouring press as she swept into Number Ten. Where did Princess Di get her hats? She must find out.

Sunshine, physical exercise, and dreams of glory. Alice was often to look back on that afternoon as the last golden period of her existence.

The sun burned down behind the mountains, making them two-dimensional cardboard mountains from a stage set. The clear air was scented with thyme and sage and pine.

To Alice's joy, Daphne had been suffering from mild sunstroke and had been taken back to the hotel by Heather. So she was allowed to ride home with Jeremy.

There is nothing more sensuous than a rich fast car driven by a rich slow man through a Highland evening.

Alice felt languorous and sexy. The setting sun flashed between the trees and bushes as they drove along with the pale gold brilliance of the far north.

The grass was so very green in this evening light, this gloaming. Green as the fairy stories, green and gold as Never-Never Land. Alice could well understand now why the Highlanders believed in fairies. Jeremy slowed the car outside the village as the tall blonde Alice had seen with Constable Macbeth came striding along the side of the road with two Irish wolfhounds on the leash.

"That's the love of Constable Macbeth's life," said Alice, delighted to have a piece of gossip.

"No hope there," said Jeremy, cheerfully and unconsciously quoting Lady Jane. "That's Priscilla Halburton-Smythe, daughter of Colonel James Halburton-Smythe. Her photograph was in *Country Life* the other week. The Halburton-Smythes own most of the land around here."

"Oh," said Alice, feeling a certain kinship with the village constable. "Perhaps she loves him too."

"She wouldn't be so silly," said Jeremy. "I wouldn't even have a chance there."

"Do people's backgrounds matter a great deal to you?" asked Alice in a low voice.

Jeremy reminded himself of his future as a politician. "No," he said stoutly. "I think all that sort of thing is rot. A lady is a lady no matter what her background."

Alice gave him a brilliant smile, and he smiled back, thinking she really was a very pretty little thing.

The sun disappeared as they plunged down to Lochdubh. Alice prayed that Jeremy would stop the car and kiss her again, but he seemed to have become immersed in his own thoughts.

When they arrived at the hotel, it was to find the rest of the fishing party surrounding Major Peter Frame. He was proudly holding up a large salmon while Heather took his photograph. Two more giants lay in plastic bags on the ground at his feet.

"How on earth did you do it?" said Jeremy, slapping the major on the back. "Hey, that fellow's got a chunk out the side."

" 'Fraid that's where I wrenched the hook out, old man," said the major. "Got too excited."

"Gosh, I wish I had stayed with you," said Jeremy. "But I thought you went off somewhere else. Did you?"

The major laid his finger alongside his nose. "Mum's the word, and talking about mum, the filthy Iron Curtain champers is on me tonight."

"Let's take them to the scales and log your catch in the book," said John, his face radiant. The photograph would go to the local papers and the fishing magazines. He loved it when one of his pupils made a good catch. And no one had ever had such luck as this before.

They all were now looking forward to the evening, reminding themselves that that was the time when Lady Jane could be guaranteed to be at her best. They were to meet in the bar at eight to toast the major's catch.

Alice slaved over her appearance. She had bought one good dinner gown at an elegant Help the Aged shop in Mayfair. Although the clothes were second-hand, most of them had barely been worn and the dinner gown was as good as new. It was made of black silk velvet, very severe, cut low in the front and slit up to mid-thigh on either side of the narrow skirt.

She was ready at last, half an hour too early. This was one time Alice was determined to make an appearance. Her high-heeled black sandals with thin straps gave her extra height and extra confidence. In the shaded light of the hotel room, her reflection looked poised and sophisticated.

Alice was just turning away from the mirror when all the barbed remarks Lady Jane had made seemed to clamour in her brain. It was no use pretending otherwise; Lady Jane had set out to find out something about each one of them. Jeremy must never know. The future Prime Minister of Britain could not have a wife with a criminal record. But then, Lady Jane knew something about Jeremy. Had he seduced a servant? But that was an upper-class sin and therefore forgivable, thought Alice miserably. She sat down on the edge of the bed and looked about her with bleak eyes.

How perfectly splendid it would be to go back to Mr. Patterson-James and hand in her notice, and say she was going to be married to Jeremy Blythe—"one of the Somerset Blythes, you know." There was Mum and Dad in Liverpool to cope with. Alice thought of her small, poky, shabby, comfortable home. Jeremy must never be allowed to go there. Mum and Dad would just have to travel to London for the wedding.

But between Alice and all those dreams stood Lady Jane. A wave of hate for Jane Winters engulfed Alice; primitive, naked hate.

Ten past eight! Alice leapt to her feet with an anguished look at her travel alarm.

The bar was crowded when she made her entrance. "Dear me, the Merry Widow," remarked Lady Jane, casting a pale look over Alice's black velvet gown. The fishing party had taken a table by the window where the major was cheerfully dispensing champagne. Alice's entrance had fallen flat because the major was describing how he had landed his first salmon, and everyone was hanging on his every word. "It's almost a good enough story to be true," said Lady Jane.

"Well, obviously it's true," said the major, his good humour unimpaired. "Here I am and there are my fish, all waiting in the hotel freezer to be smoked. By the way, Alice, your trout's still there. You forgot to have it for breakfast."

"You and Alice have a lot in common," said Lady Jane sweetly. "I can see that by the end of the week that hotel freezer will be *packed* with fish that neither of you caught."

The rest of the group tried to ignore Lady Jane's remark. "Tell us where exactly you caught those salmon, Major," asked Jeremy.

"Yes, do tell," echoed Daphne. "It isn't fair to keep such a prize place to yourself."

The major laughed and shook his head.

"Oh, *I'll* tell you," said Lady Jane. She was wearing a sort of flowered pyjama suit of the type that used to be in vogue in the thirties. Vermillion lipstick accentuated the petulant droop of her mouth. "I was talking to Ian Morrison, the ghillie, a little while ago and the dear man was in his cups and told me *exactly* how you caught them."

An awful silence fell on the group. The major stood with a bottle of champagne in one hand and a glass in the other and a silly smile pasted on his face.

"I think we should go in to dinner," said Heather loudly and clearly.

"I say, yes, let's," said the major eagerly.

They all rose to their feet. Lady Jane remained seated, a gilt sandal swinging from one plump foot as she looked up at them.

"Major Frame didn't catch those fish at all," she said with hideous clarity. "Ian Morrison took him up to the high pools on the Anstey. In one of those pools, three salmon had been trapped because of the river dwindling suddenly in the heat. They were dying from lack of oxygen. One was half out of the water and a seagull had torn a gash in its side, *not* the dear major's fictitious hook!"

One by one they filed into the dining room, not looking at each other, not looking at the major. Alice couldn't bear it any longer. She took a seat by the major. "I don't believe a word of it," she said, patting his hand. "That terrible woman made it all up."

The major smiled at her in a rigid sort of way and drank steadily from his champagne glass.

Charlie Baxter had been invited to join them for

dinner. He had not been in the bar and therefore did not know about the major's humiliation. But he looked from face to face and then settled down to eat his food so that he could escape as quickly as possible.

Lady Jane launched into her usual evening flow of anecdotes while the rest stared at her with hate-filled eyes.

What the major had done was not so bad. Alice thought he had been very clever. She herself, she was sure, would have sworn blind she had caught them.

Heather Cartwright was miserable. She had already posted off the photographs, developed quickly by John in their own darkroom, to the local papers and fishing magazines. Heather didn't know which one she wanted to kill—Lady Jane or the major. When it had seemed as if the major had landed that splendid catch, Heather and John had heaved a sigh of relief. Surely nothing Lady Jane said could touch them now. It was the most marvellous piece of publicity for the fishing school. But the silly, vain major had now played right into Lady Jane's hands. Well *I* can just about bear it, thought Heather, but if anything happens to this fishing school, it will kill John.

"I always think those silly beanpole women who

model clothes are a hoot," Lady Jane was saying. "I remember going to Hartnell's collection and there were the usual pan-faced lot of mannequins modelling clothes for the Season and the salon was so hot and stuffy and we were all half asleep. They were marching on saying in those awful sort of Putney deb voices, 'For Goodwood, For Ascot', and things like that, and then this one marches on and says, 'For Cowes', and we all laughed fit to burst." Lady Jane herself laughed in a fat, jolly way.

Marvin Roth was gloomily longing for the appearance of that village constable with the red hair. No one else seemed to have the courage to be rude to Lady Jane. If she did know something about him, Marvin Roth, then good luck to her. But that remark of hers to the constable about "having power" was worrying. What sort of power?

Blackmail, thought Marvin Roth suddenly. That's it. And there was nothing he could do about it. Had they been in New York, then things might have been different. There was always someone who could be hired to clear away people like Lady Jane . . . although he had heard that even in old New York things were not what they were in the early seventies, say, when a thousand dollars to the local Mafia could get someone wasted. If only he could do it himself. Maybe he should just try to pay her off before she approached him. Amy must never know. Amy was the prize. In order to get divorced from that little whore of a first wife, he had paid an arm and a leg, but gaining Amy Blanchard had been worth it. He knew Amy hoped he would make it big on the political scene. Of course, Amy either knew or had guessed about his unsavoury past, but any approach to Lady Jane must be kept secret. There was a vein of steel running through Amy, and he was sure she would despise him for trying to conciliate Lady Jane.

Marvin polished his bald head with his hand and looked sideways at Lady Jane. No ma'am, he thought, the day I let a broad like you screw up my act, well, you can kiss my ass in Macy's window.

At last the horrible dinner was over. Alice smoothed down the velvet of her gown with a nervous hand and smiled hopefully at Jeremy. He looked at her vaguely and turned abruptly to Daphne Gore. "Come on," he said to Daphne. "We've got to talk."

Alice's eyes filmed over with tears. She was dreadfully tired. She felt alien, foreign, alone. When she passed the bar, it was full of people drinking and laughing, the other guests who did not belong to the fishing school. She hesitated, longing for the courage to go in and join them, longing for just one compliment on her gown to make some of her misery go away.

CONSTABLE HAMISH MACBETH leaned on his garden gate and gazed across the loch to the lights of the hotel. He had fed the chickens and geese; his dog lay at his feet, stretched across his boots like a carriage rug, snoring peacefully.

Hamish lit a cigarette and pushed his cap back on his head. He was not happy, which was a fairly unusual state of mind for him. This was usually the time of the day he liked best.

He had to admit to himself he had let Lady Jane get under his skin. He did not like the idea of that fat woman ferreting out details of his family life, even if there was nothing shameful to ferret out.

It was true that Hamish Macbeth had six brothers and sisters to support. He had been born one year after his parents had been married. After that there had been a long gap and then Mr. and Mrs. Macbeth had produced three boys and three girls in as quick a succession as was physically possible. As in many Celtic families, it was taken for granted that the eldest son would remain a bachelor until such time as the next in line were able to support themselves. Hamish had deliberately chosen the unambitious career of village constable because it enabled him to send most of his pay home. He was a skilful poacher and presents of venison and salmon found their way regularly to his parents' croft in Ross and Cromarty. The little egg money he got from his poultry was sent home as well. Then there was the annual prize money for best hill runner at the Strathbane Highland games. Hamish had taken the prize five years in a row.

His father was a crofter but could not make nearly enough to support all six younger children. Hamish had accepted his lot as he accepted most things, with easy-going good nature.

But of late, he had found himself wishing he had a little bit more money in his pocket and yet he would not admit to himself the reason for this.

What he *could* admit to himself was that he was very worried about the fishing class. Crime in Hamish's parish usually ran to things like bigamy or the occasional drunk on a Saturday night. Most village wrangles were settled out of court, so to speak, by the diplomatic Hamish. He was not plagued with the savage violence of poaching gangs, although he felt sure that would come. A new housing estate was being built outside the village; one of those mad schemes where the worst of the welfare cases were wrenched out of the cosy clamour of the city slums and transported to the awesome bleakness of the

Highlands. To Hamish, these housing estates were the breeding grounds of poaching gangs who dynamited the salmon to the surface and fought each other with razors and sharpened bicycle chains.

Something in his bones seemed to tell him that trouble was going to come from this fishing class. He decided it was time to find out a little more about Lady Jane.

He sifted through the filing cabinet of his mind, which was filled with the names and addresses and telephone numbers of various friends and relatives. Like most Highlanders, Hamish had relatives scattered all over the world.

Then he remembered his second cousin, Rory Grant, who worked for the *Daily Recorder* in Fleet Street. Hamish ambled indoors and put through a collect call. "This is Constable Macbeth of Lochdubh with a verra important story for Rory Grant," said Hamish when the newspaper switchboard showed signs of being reluctant to pay for the call. When he was at last put through to Rory, Hamish gave a description of Lady Jane Winters and asked for details about her.

"I'll need to go through to the library and look at her cuttings," said Rory. "It might take a bit of time. I'll call you back."

"Och, no," said Hamish comfortably, "I am not

paying for the call, so I will just hold on and have a beer while you are looking."

"Suit yourself," said Rory. Hamish tucked the phone under one ear and fished a bottle of beer out of his bottom drawer. He did not like cold beer and, in any case, Hamish had grown up on American movies where the hero had fished a bottle out of his desk drawer, and had never got over the thrill of being able to do the same thing, even though it was warm beer and not bourbon.

He had left the police office door open, and a curious hen came hopping in, flew up on top of the typewriter, and stared at him with curious, beady eyes.

Priscilla Halburton-Smythe suddenly appeared in the doorway, a brace of grouse dangling from one hand, and smiled at the sight of Hamish with his huge boots on the desk, bottle of beer in one hand, phone in the other and hen in front.

"I see you're interviewing one of the village criminals," said Priscilla.

"Not I," said Hamish. "I am waiting for my cousin in London to come back to the telephone with some vital information."

"I meant the hen, silly. Joke. I've brought you some grouse."

"Have they been hung?"

."No, I shot them today. Why do you ask?"

"Oh, nothing, nothing. It is verra kind of you, Miss Halburton-Smythe."

Since Hamish's family did not like grouse, the policeman was calculating how soon he could manage to get into Ullapool, where he would no doubt get a good price for the brace from one of the butchers. If they were fresh, that would give him a few days. Hamish did not possess a freezer except the small compartment in his refrigerator, which was full of TV dinners.

Hamish stood up, startling the hen, who flew off with a squawk, and pulled out a chair for Priscilla. He studied her as she sat down. She was wearing a beige silk blouse tucked into cord breeches. Her waist was small and her breasts high and firm. The pale oval of her face, framed by the pale gold of her hair, was saved from being insipid by a pair of bright blue eyes fringed with sooty lashes. He cleared his throat. "I cannot leave the telephone. But you will find a bottle of beer in the refrigerator in the kitchen."

"I thought you didn't like cold beer," called Priscilla over her shoulder as she made her way across the tiny hall to the kitchen. "I aye keep one for the guests," called Hamish, thinking wistfully that he had kept a cold bottle of beer especially for her since that golden day she had first dropped in to see him about a minor poaching matter four whole months ago.

"No more trouble, I hope," added Hamish as Priscilla returned with a foaming glass. "I hope it is not the crime that brings you here."

"No, I thought you might like some birds for the pot." Priscilla leaned back and crossed her legs, tightening the material along her thighs by the movement. Hamish half closed his eyes.

"Actually, I'm escaping," said Priscilla. "Daddy's brought the most awful twit up from London. He wants me to marry him."

"And will you?"

"No, you silly constable. Didn't I just say he was a twit? I say, there's a picture show on at the village hall tonight. Second showing, ten o'clock. Wouldn't it be a shriek if we went to it?"

Hamish smiled. "My dear lassie, it is Bill Haley and his Comets in *Rock Around the Clock*, which was showing a wee bit before you were born, I'm thinking."

"Lovely. Let's go after whoever you're speaking to speaks."

"I cannot think Colonel Halburton-Smythe would like his daughter to go to the pictures with the local bobby."

"He won't know."

"You have not been long in the Highlands. Give it a day, give it a week, everyone around here knows everything."

"But Daddy doesn't *speak* to anyone in the village."

"Your housemaid, Maisie, is picture daft. She'll be there. She'll tell the other servants and that po-faced butler, Jenkins, will see it as his duty to inform the master."

"Do you care?"

"Not much," grinned Hamish. "Oh, Rory, it is yourself."

He listened intently. Priscilla watched Hamish's face, noticing for the first time how cat-like his hazel eyes looked with their Celtic narrowness at the outer edges.

"Thank you, Rory," said Hamish finally. "That is verra interesting. I am surprised that fact about her is not better known."

The voice quacked again.

"Thank you," said Hamish gloomily. "I may be in the way of having to report a wee murder to you in the next few days. No, it is chust my joke, Rory." Hamish's accent became more sibilant and Highland when he was seriously upset.

He put down the phone and stared into space.

"What was all that about?" asked Priscilla curiously.

"Gossip about a gossip," said Hamish, getting to his feet. "Wait and I'll just lock up, Miss Halburton-Smythe, and we'll be on our way. I'll tell you about it one of these days."

Day Four

Above all, when playing a big fish, stay calm.
—Peter Wheat, *The Observer's Book of Fly Fishing*

It was a very subdued party that met in the lounge in the morning. Heather Cartwright was visibly losing her usual phlegmatic calm. Her plump face was creased with worry, and her voice shook as she asked them to be seated.

Lady Jane was absent, but everyone seemed to jump a little when anyone entered the room. John Cartwright, in a weary voice, said he felt they had not all learnt the art of casting properly and so he would take them out to the lawn at the back to give a demonstration. His eyes turned to the major to make his usual remark, that those with experience could go ahead, but somehow he could not bring himself to say anything.

They stood about him, shivering in the chill,

misty morning air as he demonstrated how to make the perfect cast. He warmed to his subject but his little audience fidgetted restlessly and moved from foot to foot.

Finally, their unease reached him, and he stopped his lecture with a little sigh. "Enough from me," he said. "We will go to the upper reaches of the river Anstey. I'll leave word at the desk for Lady Jane. There is no point in disturbing her if she's sleeping late."

Like the day before, the warmth of the sun began to penetrate the mist. "Bad day for fishing," said the major knowledgeably, and Alice could only envy the quick way in which he had recovered from his humiliation.

"I like the sunshine," she said, and then could not resist adding, "and I hope Lady Jane doesn't turn up to spoil it."

"Got a feeling we won't be seeing her," said the major cheerfully.

And then it was as if they all had the same feeling. Everyone's spirits began to lift. John Cartwright smiled at his wife and pressed her hand as he drove up the twists and winds to the river. "I've a feeling we've been worrying too much about that woman," he murmured to Heather. "Don't worry. I'll see to it she doesn't plague us anymore."

Alice gave a little sigh of relief. Obviously the Cartwrights were going to tell Lady Jane to leave. She grinned at Charlie, but Charlie was looking white and sick and turned his head away.

She shrugged. Again, the sunshine was bleaching away the worries of the night. She was prepared to accept that she did not stand a chance with Jeremy. Let him have Daphne. There was no use fighting it. She would enjoy the exercise and scenery as much as she could. Once more her thoughts returned to Mr. Patterson-James. She was sure he would be impressed when she described her holiday.

But when she climbed out of the car and waited for Heather to hand her her rod, she could not help wishing Jeremy would join her as he had done on the other days.

But John Cartwright, with the continued absence of Lady Jane, was once more on form. He was determined his little class should get the proper schooling. He said he was going to give them a demonstration of how to catch a salmon. When they all had their gear on he led the way up a twisting path beside the river at a smart trot. Alice felt the sweat beginning to trickle down her face as she stumbled along after him. Below them, at the bottom of the steep bank, the river Anstey foamed and frothed. At times, delicate strands of silver birch and alder and hazel screened the river from their view, and then, around another turn it would appear again, tumbling headlong on its way to the sea. To the right, the tangled forest climbed up the mountainside.

Marvin Roth put an arm around his wife's shoulders to help her. "Didn't mean to take you on a survival course," he said. Amy shook his arm away and strode ahead of him up the path with long, athletic strides. Marvin hesitated, took off his cap, and passed a hand over the dome of his bald head. Then he replaced his cap and plunged after her.

"What's up with you this morning, Miss Alice?" came Jeremy's voice behind Alice. "Don't I get a smile?"

Remember, it's no use, Alice chided herself fiercely. Aloud she said, "I haven't any energy to do anything other than try to keep up. It's so *hot*. I didn't think the Scottish Highlands would be so hot."

"It's like this sometimes," said Jeremy, falling into step beside her. He was wearing a blue cotton shirt open at the neck, as blue as the sky above. He smelled of clean linen, aftershave, and masculine sweat. The heavy gold band of his wrist watch lay against the brand-new tan of his arm. Alice's good resolutions began to fade.

"What did you think about our major's little trick?" Jeremy went on. "Not quite the manner of the officer or the gentleman, as our Lady Jane would point out."

"I think it was understandable," said Alice. "It must have been a terrible temptation to lie. Only think the way people go on about cars and horses and...boats. It's surely more in the nature of a gentleman to *lie* when it comes to sports."

She gave Jeremy a rather hard-eyed stare. Alice's better nature was trying to drive him away, but Jeremy only felt she had gone off him and was a little piqued.

"Didn't *you* lie yourself?" he jeered. "Our gossip accused you of lying about the fish you were *supposed* to have caught."

Easy tears rushed to Alice's eyes. "I think you're horrid. How can you accuse me of such a thing?"

"Hey, steady on!" Jeremy caught her arm. "There's no need to fly off the handle like that."

"I don't know what's up with me," said Alice, scrubbing her eyes with the back of her hand. "I think it's that Jane female. She's always hinting things in a spiteful sort of way."

"You know," said Jeremy, taking Alice's hand in a warm clasp. "I don't think we'll ever see her again. I feel she's taken the hint and left. No one can be that thick-skinned—it surely got through to her that not one of us can stand her."

He gave her hand a squeeze. Alice's mercurial spirits soared, and her resolution to forget about Jeremy whirled up to the summer sky and disappeared. After they had been climbing about a mile, and Amy Roth was loudly and clearly threatening to call it a day and turn back, John finally came to a stop. "Down here to the Keeper's Pool," he called, "and be very quiet." The tangled undergrowth gave way at their side of the pool where a ledge of flat rocks hung over the water. The pool swirled and boiled like a witch's cauldron.

It was a joy to watch John casting. He did a roll cast across the pool, landing the fly delicately on the surface. All at once, fishing fever gripped John and he forgot about his class. Suddenly, with a flash of silver scales, a salmon leapt high in the air. Alice clapped her hands in excitement, and everyone said, "Shhhhh."

Now the whole class was as intense as their teacher. Then, just as John was casting, Charlie slipped and nearly fell into the pool. Heather shouted, "Look out!" and caught his arm. John turned to make sure the boy was safe, leaving his line tumbling and turning in the water.

He turned back once he had assured himself that

Charlie was all right. He flicked at his line and his rod began to bend. "You've got one," breathed the major.

"I don't know...I think it's a rock," muttered John. He moved to another angle and tried to reel in his line. He had something heavy on the end of it, something that was twisting and turning.

His heart began to beat hard. Of course, if it wasn't a rock, it could be a sunken branch, twisting and turning in the churning of the water. He moved back round to where the group was standing on the beach of rocks. Underneath the rock shelf the water was clear and still, a little island of calm just outside the churning of the pool.

He reeled in again, feeling his excitement fade as whatever it was that he had hooked moved from the turbulent water into the still shallows. A log, he thought.

And then Daphne Gore, the usually cool and unflappable Daphne, began to scream and scream, harsh, terror-stricken screams tearing apart the sylvan picture of pretty woods, singing birds, and tumbling water.

Alice stared down into the golden water directly below her feet as she stood on the ledge. And Lady Jane stared back.

Slowly rising to the surface came the bloated,

distorted features of Lady Jane Winters. Her tongue was sticking out, and her blue eyes bulged and glared straight up into the ring of faces.

"She must have hit her head and fallen in," whispered Alice, clinging to Jeremy.

John waded into the water, heaved the body up, and then let it fall with a splash. He turned a chalk-white face up to Heather. "Get Macbeth," he said. "Get the police."

"But didn't she just fall?" asked Heather, as white as her husband.

John prodded at Lady Jane's fat neck. "There's a leader round her neck. She's been strangled. And look." He pointed to Lady Jane's legs.

"Oh, God," said Alice, "there's chains wrapped round them."

"She could have done it herself," said Amy Roth through white lips. "Marvin. Help me. I feel sick."

"Get the police, dammit," shouted John. "And get that child out of here. The rest, stay where you are."

"If it's murder, we'd better all stay," said Marvin, holding Amy tightly against him.

"Don't be silly," said Heather. "It took someone powerful to overcome a woman like Lady Jane and strangle her with a leader. Come along, Charlie. I'll take you to your aunt's and then I'll bring Constable Macbeth."

"Take me to your leader," said Daphne and began to giggle.

"Can't anyone stop her?" pleaded Amy.

"Pull yourself together, Daphne," snapped John Cartwright.

"Steady the buffs," urged the major.

Daphne sat down abruptly, pulled out a gold cigarette case, and extracted a cigarette with hands that trembled so much the cigarettes spilled out on the rock. Jeremy stooped to help her. Their eyes met and held in a long stare.

"Go up the hill and wait at the top," commanded John. "I'll stay with the body."

Alice, Jeremy, Daphne, the major, and Marvin and Amy Roth made their way up the path. They moved, bunched together, along the upper path until it opened out into a small glade. They sat down in silence. Major Peter Frame pulled out a packet of cigarettes and offered them around.

Marvin was the first to speak. "I always knew that dame was a party pooper," he said gloomily. "She's worse dead than alive. She was murdered, of course."

"Well, it wasn't any of us," said Alice. She tried to speak bravely, but her voice trembled and she rubbed at the gooseflesh on her arms.

"Yeah, she was the sort of woman *anyone* would

have murdered, I reckon," said Amy Roth shakily. "Was she rich? Maybe one of her relatives followed her up here and bumped her off."

"By Jove, I think you're right," the major chimed in eagerly. "I mean *de mortuis* and all that, but she was a really repulsive, nasty woman. Look at the way she kept getting at each of us. Stands to reason she'd been doing the same thing to other people for years."

"I suppose the holiday's over," said Daphne, looking once more her calm self. "I mean, what's going to happen to us?"

"It won't be left to Macbeth, not a murder," said Jeremy. "They'll be sending in some of the big brass. I s'pose they'll take statements from us, take a note of our home addresses, and let us go."

"It's so unfair," drawled Daphne. "Just as I was getting the hang of this fishing thing. You know, I felt so sure that today would be the day I would catch something."

Everyone looked at Daphne with approval. They were not only joined by the tragedy of the murder but bound in fellowship by that old-as-time obsession, the lure of the kill.

"Well, I've paid for this week and I jolly well expect to get full value," said the major, "or they'll need to give me my money back. As soon as that oaf of a village copper gets our statements, I'm off to spend the rest of the day fishing, and if John Cartwright isn't up to it, I'll take any of you as pupils if you'll have me."

"I'll go with you for a start," said Jeremy, and the others nodded. The major might have lied about his magnificent salmon bag, but he was undoubtedly an expert angler. His line never became tangled in bushes, and he made his own flies, several of which flaunted their garish colours on his hat.

"I thought of killing her," said Alice suddenly. "I'm *glad* she's dead, and I feel guilty at the same time. I feel I *wished* her to death."

There was a shocked silence.

"Well," said Jeremy uncomfortably, "may as well be honest. I think we all felt like that."

"Not me," said Amy Roth. The skin at the corners of her eyelids had a stretched, almost oriental look. "We Blanchards are made of pretty strong stuff."

"Tell us about it," said Daphne harshly. "Tell us about the bloody ol' plantation and massah's in de col', col' ground. Tell us anything in the world, but don't talk about the murder."

"Not if you're going to be rude," said Amy, leaning against her husband's shoulder and seeking his hand for comfort.

"I didn't mean to be rude. I really would like to hear about it. All I can think of is a sort of *Gone With the Wind* setting, all crinolines and mint juleps."

Amy laughed. "Believe it or not, it was a little bit like that. Of course, that life all went when I was still a child. Pa was a gambler in the true Southern tradition. Well, lemme see. It was a big barn of a place, the Blanchard mansion, like you see in the movies. Pillared colonial front, wide verandahs all round. Green shutters, cool rooms smelling of beeswax and lavender. Flowers evvywheah," said Amy, becoming Southern in accent as she warmed to her subject. Amy's normal voice was a light, almost Bostonian accent. "And antiques! I decleah, there were more Chippendales and whatyoucallums there than you'd get in one of your English stately homes. We hud been importing them for yeahs."

"Listen!" The major put a hand to his ear in a sort of list-who-approacheth way. Most of his gestures were stagey.

Heather appeared with Constable Macbeth behind her. The policeman was wearing his usual black uniform, shiny with wear. He pulled off his cap, and his red hair blazed in the sun like fire. It was that true Highland red that sometimes looked as if it has purple lights.

"I will chust go down and look at the body," he said placidly. "There will be detectives coming up from Strathbane by this afternoon, but I must make sure nothing is touched. If you will wait where you are, I will return in a wee moment and take the statements."

They waited now in silence. A little knot of dread was beginning to form in the pit of each stomach. It had just been becoming comfortably unreal. Now reality was with them in the shape of the village constable who was down at the pool bent over the body.

A small, fussy man erupted into the glade and glared about him. "Dr. MacArthur," said Heather, "I'll take you down. Mr. Macbeth is with the body now."

"The procurator fiscal is on his way from Strathbane," said the doctor. "But I may as well make a preliminary examination. Macbeth's talking about murder. But the man's havering. She could have got her own leader wrapped around her neck and fallen into the pool."

"And wrapped chains around her legs to sink her?" said Marvin Roth dryly.

"Eh, what? Better go and see."

He disappeared with Heather.

Again, the group waited.

"I'm hungry," said Alice at last. "I know I shouldn't

feel hungry, but I am. Would it be too awful if we went back to the cars and had something to eat?"

"Better wait," said the major. "Can't be very long now."

But it seemed ages. They could hear people coming and going. The sun was very high in the sky, and flies droned and danced in the green quiet of the glade.

At last, Hamish Macbeth appeared looking hot and grim.

"We'll all just be going back to the hotel," he said. "I'm getting this path closed off until the big brass arrives. The water bailiffs have said they will stand guard."

A moment before, each one of them had felt he would give anything to be able to move. Now they were overcome by a strange reluctance. There was one large fact each of them had to face up to sooner or later, and each one was putting off the moment.

They all gathered in the hotel lounge. Constable Macbeth surveyed them solemnly.

"The manager has given me the use of the wee room off the reception, so I'll take you one at a time. You first, Mr. Cartwright."

"I'll come too," said Heather quickly.

"No need for that," said the constable easily. "This way, Mr. Cartwright."

Heather sat down, flushed with distress. She looked like a mother seeing her youngest off to boarding school for the first time.

John followed Hamish Macbeth into a small, dark room furnished simply with a scarred wooden desk, some old filing cabinets, and two hard chairs. Hamish sat down behind the desk, and John took the chair opposite.

"Now," said the policeman, producing a large notebook, "we'll make a start. It is the doctor's guess that Lady Jane was in the water all night. When did you last see her?"

"At dinner last night," said John. "We were celebrating the major's catch."

"Or rather, the major's find," murmured Hamish. "And was she wearing then what she was wearing when she was found dead?"

"Yes, I mean no. No, she was wearing a flowery trouser suit thing last night with evening sandals. She seemed to be wearing her usual fishing outfit when . . . when we saw her in the pool."

Hamish made a note and then looked up. "Did you know Lady Jane's job?"

"Job?" said John. "I didn't know she worked."

"Well, we'll leave that until later. Did your wife know the nature of Lady Jane's job, I wonder?"

A faint line of sweat glistened on John's upper

lip. There was a silence. Hamish patiently repeated the question.

"No," said John, suddenly and savagely. "Look here, Macbeth, what is this? You know us both. Do you think either of us would kill her?"

"That is not for me to say," said Hamish. "But I willnae get to the person who did it if I don't start to eliminate those that did not. Now what were you doing late last night?"

"How late?"

"She was last seen going up to her room at ten-thirty, according to the hotel servants."

"I went to bed," said John, "and Heather too. We'd had a fairly exhausting day."

"Did anyone in the group seem to hate Lady Jane?"

"No, we all loved her," said John sarcastically. "Good God, man, use your wits. Nobody liked her, not even you."

"Mphmm. Lady Jane had a nasty habit of making remarks. Did she say anything to you?"

"Nothing in particular. Just general carping."

"Aye, well, that will do for now. If you'll just send Mrs. Cartwright in."

As John entered the room, Alice was saying with a nervous giggle, "Just think. One of us must have killed her. I mean, it stands to reason..."

It was out in the open now, put into words; that thought they had been keeping resolutely at bay since Lady Jane's body was discovered.

"He wants to see you," said John to Heather. He added in a low voice as he held open the door for her, "I told him we didn't know what she did."

The door to the lounge opened, and a small, anxious-looking woman dressed in a lumpy, powder-blue dress fussed in, dragging Charlie with her. "I'm Mrs. Baxter, Tina Baxter," she announced, staring around the room with rather bulging blue eyes. "I only arrived today. My poor boy." She tried to hug Charlie, but he flinched away from this public demonstration of maternal affection.

"You should keep the boy away from this," said John. "There was no need to bring him along."

"There was every need," said Tina Baxter. "I was told the police wanted to interrogate the whole fishing class and nobody is going to frighten my little boy with a lot of questions."

She proceeded to tell the bemused company about her divorce and the difficulties of rearing a boy single-handed, and that Charlie had written to her saying this Lady Jane was a cruel and evil woman. Her words began to tumble out one over the other in an increasingly unintelligible stream.

Then she stopped suddenly and stared at the

door with her mouth open. Hamish's big brass had arrived from Strathbane.

A big, heavyset man draped in a grey double-breasted suit introduced himself as Detective Chief Inspector Blair. He was flanked by two other detectives, Jimmy Anderson and Harry MacNab. Jimmy Anderson was thin and wiry with suspicious blue eyes, and MacNab was short and dumpy with thick black hair and wet-looking black eyes.

"Which one of you runs this school?" demanded Mr Blair. He spoke with a thick Glaswegian accent.

"I do," said John. "Constable Macbeth is talking to my wife at the moment."

"Where?"

"In there," said John. "I'll show you the way."

"No need," said Blair. "We'll introduce ourselves."

Hamish got to his feet as the three men entered the small office. Heather gratefully escaped.

"Macbeth, is it?" said Blair, sitting down in the chair Hamish had just vacated. "We've got a real juicy one here. Bit out of your league, Constable. The boys and the forensic team are combing the ground. Good bit of work on your part to get the water bailiffs to stand guard."

He smiled at Hamish and waited for a look of gratitude to appear on the constable's face at the compliment. Hamish looked stolidly back, and Blair scowled with irritation.

"Yes, well, I suppose they all know they're supposed to stay put until I'm satisfied that no one in this school did it. School, indeed. All that money and fuss just to catch a fish."

"I think it would be better if I told them they are not to leave Lochdubh at the moment," said Hamish. "Them not having the ESP."

"Enough of that," snapped Blair. "Before I have the rest in, what do you think the motive was for this murder?"

"I think it had something to do with Lady Jane's job," said Hamish slowly.

"Job? What job?"

"Lady Jane Winters was, in fact, Jane Maxwell, columnist for the London *Evening Star*."

"That rag! Well, what's so bad about being a columnist?"

"I understand she specialized in taking holidays where there were going to be small groups of British people. She would find out something nasty about each one, since she liked to prove that everyone has a skeleton in the closet. There have been complaints to the press council, but her column's been too popular. Folks chust lap it up and think it will never happen to them. Maybe someone in this group knew about her column, although the fact that she was Jane Maxwell was kept a closely guarded secret."

"And how did *you* find out if it's that much of a secret?" asked Blair, his eyes raking over the lanky length of the village constable.

"I haff my methods, Watson," grinned Hamish.

"I am not putting up with any cheek from a Highlander," snarled Blair. "How did you find out?"

"I have a relative that works in Fleet Street."

"And which of these fishing lot knew about her being Jane Maxwell?"

"I do not know," said Hamish patiently. "I was just beginning to find out when you arrived. I have talked with John Cartwright and you interrupted me when I was in the process of talking to Mrs Heather Cartwright."

"Before I start with the rest, I'd better fix up accommodation for me and my men. I'll stay here myself, but it's a bit pricey for the lot of us. We've got five officers combing the bushes along with the forensic team at the moment. I saw that police station of yours. You do yourself very well. Any chance of a spare bed or two?"

"I have not the room. I have the one bed for myself and the other bedroom has not the bed but the gardening stuff and the poultry feed and the bags of fertilizer..."

"Okay, okay, spare me the rural details." Blair looked piercingly at Hamish, who gave him a sweet smile.

Simple, thought Blair. Would have to be to live here all year round.

He placed his beefy hands on the desk and looked at Hamish in a kindly way. "I'm thinking you're a wee bit too inexperienced for this sort of high-class crime," he said. "We'll use your office at the station because I'm damned if I'll pay hotel phone prices. I have to fight hard enough to get my expenses as it is. Just you attend to your usual rounds and leave the detective work to us. We're all experienced men."

Hamish looked at the detective chief inspector blankly. Only a few minutes before he had been wondering how to keep out of the case. He had taken a dislike to the chief detective and his side-kicks and did not want to tag around after them. But now he had been told to keep clear, well, all that did was give him a burning desire to find out who had killed Lady Jane.

"I'll be off then," said Hamish. Blair watched him go and shook his head sadly. "Poor fellow," he said. "Never had to do any real work in his life before, and, like all these Highlanders, fights shy of it as much as possible. Send in that American couple, MacNab. Typical pair of tourists. May as well get rid of them first."

HAMISH AMBLED ALONG the front, gazing dreamily out over the loch. The early evening sun was flooding the bay with gold. A pair of seals were rolling and turning lazily, sending golden ripples washing about the white hulls of the yachts and the green and black hulls of the fishing boats.

He saw the slim, elegant figure of Priscilla Halburton-Smythe walking towards him, and, suddenly overcome with a mixture of shyness and longing, he stopped and leaned his elbows on the mossy stone wall above the beach.

She stopped and stood beside him. "What's all this I hear?" said Priscilla. "The hillside's crawling with bobbies, putting things in plastic bags."

"Lady Jane Winters has been murdered."

"I heard something to that effect. Big, fat, nasty woman, wasn't she?"

"Aye, you could say that."

"And who did it, Holmes?"

"I chust don't know, and I've been more or less told to go home and feed my chickens by the detectives from Strathbane."

"Well, you must be pleased about that. I mean,

you never were exactly one of the world's greatest workers."

"How would you know that, Miss Halburton-Smythe? It is not as if I have the murder on my hands every day of the week."

"You must admit when Daddy wants to talk to you about poaching or something, you're never where you should be. I told Daddy not to worry you about poachers since you're one yourself."

"That is not a very nice thing to say."

"I was only joking. Do you really want to find the murderer? Do you need a Watson? I shall follow you about saying, 'By Jove, you're a wonder. How on earth did you think of that?' "

"Oh, I suppose I'll do as I'm told and keep out of the way," said Hamish equably.

"Funny, I thought you'd have been dying to find out for yourself. All that Highland curiosity." Priscilla sounded disappointed.

"Aye, well..." began Hamish, and then his gaze suddenly sharpened. Mrs. Baxter and Charlie could be seen leaving the hotel.

"Are you going to ask them questions?" asked Priscilla, following his gaze. "Can I listen?"

"Och, no. The wee lad has a very interesting stamp and I wanted to have another look at it."

"Hamish Macbeth, I give you up!"

He gave her a crooked grin. "I did not know you had ever taken me on, Miss Halburton-Smythe."

He pushed his hat up on his forehead, thrust his hands in his pockets, and strolled off to meet the Baxters.

Highly irritated, Priscilla watched him go.

Day Five

*A counsel of perfection is very easy advice to
give, but is usually quite impracticable.*

—Maxwell Knight, *Bird Gardening*

Alice started to dress hurriedly, although it was
only seven in the morning. She wanted to escape
from the hotel before they were besieged by the
press again. They had started to filter in gradually,
and by late evening they had grown to an army: an
army of questioning faces. Alice's juvenile crime
loomed large in her mind. If Lady Jane could have
found out about *that*, then they could too. Normally
Alice would have been thrilled to bits at the idea
of getting her photograph in the papers. But her
murky past tortured her. Jeremy had been particularly warm and friendly to her the evening before.
She felt sure he would not even look at her again
if he found out. The major had howled at the hotel

manager over the problem of the press, and the manager had at last reluctantly banned them. He was thoroughly fed up with the notoriety the murder had brought to his hotel and had hoped to ease the pain with the large amount of money the gentlemen of the press were spending in the bar. But guests other than the major had complained, guests who came every year. And so the reporters and the photographers were now billeted out in the village, most of them at a boarding house at the other end of the bay.

Alice was just on the point of leaving the room when the telephone began to ring. She stared at it and then suddenly rushed and picked it up. Her mother's voice, sharp with agitation, sounded over the line. "What's all this, luv? Your name's in the morning papers. You didn't even tell us you was going to such a place. We're that worried."

"It's all right, Mum," said Alice. "It's got nothing to do with me."

"I know that, luv, but that woman that was murdered, her photo's in the papers and she was around here last week, asking questions. Said she was writing a piece on young girls who had made the move to London and their reasons for doing it."

She must have got all our addresses from Heather, thought Alice with a sudden sickening lurch of the heart. Heather even sent me the names of the other guests, sort of to make it sound social.

Her voice shrill with anxiety, Alice asked, "Did she find out anything about me being in court?"

"You was never in court, luv."

"Yes. 'Member? It was when I broke Mr. Jenkins' window and he took me to the juvenile court."

"Oh, *that*. She didn't ask me and I don't suppose anyone around here remembers a silly little thing like that. She talked to Maggie Harrison, mind."

Alice held tightly on to the phone. Maggie Harrison had been her rival for years. If Maggie could have remembered anything nasty about her, Alice, then Maggie would have undoubtedly told everything.

"Are you there?" Her mother's voice sounded like a squawk. "I'm in a call box and the money's running out. Can you call me back?"

"No, Mum, I've got to go. I'll be all right."

"Take care of yourself, will you? I don't like you getting mixed up with those sort of people."

The line went dead.

Alice slowly replaced the receiver and wiped her damp palm on her sweater. Well, Lady Jane couldn't write anything now.

She turned quickly and ran from the room. Outside the hotel a thin, greasy drizzle was falling.

She looked quickly along the waterfront, dreading to see a reporter waiting to pounce on her, but everything was deserted as far as she could see. She hesitated. Perhaps it would have been better to stay in the hotel. It was now banned to the press, so why bother to venture out? But the fear of anyone—Jeremy in particular—finding out about her past drove her on.

There was a pleasant smell of woodsmoke, tar, kippers, bacon and strong tea drifting from the cottages. Alice approached Constable Macbeth's house and saw him standing in his garden, feeding the chickens. He turned at the sound of her footsteps, and she smiled weakly.

"Is your third degree over?" asked the policeman.

"It wasn't so bad," said Alice. "I really didn't know that awful woman was a newspaper columnist, and I think they believed me."

"I was just about to make a cup of tea. Would you like one?"

"Yes," said Alice gratefully, thinking how very unlike a policeman Constable Macbeth looked. He was hatless and wearing an old army sweater and a faded pair of jeans. That chief detective had made it plain that the village constable would not be having anything to do with the investigation. Mr. Macbeth must have riled him in some way because he had been quite unpleasant about it, Alice remembered. Blair had asked her if she had noticed or heard anything unusual that might point to the murderer, and Alice had shaken her head, but had said if she did remember anything she would tell Constable Macbeth, and that was when Blair had sourly pointed out that the village policeman was not part of the murder investigation.

Alice followed Hamish into his kitchen, which was long and narrow with a table against the window.

She looked around the kitchen curiously. It was messy in a clean sort of way. There were piles of magazines, china, bits of old farm implements, Victorian dolls, and stacks of jam jars.

"I'm a hoarder," said Mr. Macbeth. "I aye think a thing'll fetch a good price if I just hang on to it. I have a terrible time throwing things away. Milk and sugar?"

"Yes, please," said Alice. He gave her a cup, sat down next to her at the table, and heaped five spoonfuls of sugar into his own tea.

"Do I look like a murderer?" asked Alice intently.

"I think a murderer could look like anyone," said the policeman placidly. "Now this Lady Jane, it strikes me she went to a lot of work to find out about the people who were going to be at the fishing school. How did she know who was going?"

"Oh, that's easy. Heather sent us all a list of names and addresses. The idea is that we can get in touch with anyone in our area and maybe travel up with them. That's how Jeremy came to travel up with Daphne. He didn't know her before." Alice blushed furiously and buried her nose in her cup.

"Yes, and she must have found out about me and my family after she came," said Hamish. "She had only to ask a few people in the village. You can't keep anything secret in the Highlands."

"I wish she had never come," said Alice passionately. "She's ruined my life."

"Indeed! And how is that?"

The rain was falling more steadily and the cluttered kitchen was peaceful and warm. Alice had a longing to unburden herself.

"If a young man was interested in a girl," she said, not looking at him, "would you think that young man might go off that girl if he found out she had done something...well, against the law, when she was a kid?"

"It depends on the young man. Now if you're talking about Mr. Jeremy Blythe..."

"You *noticed*. He *is* rather sweet on me." Alice removed her hat and tossed back her fluffy hair in what she fondly thought was a *femme-fataleish* sort of way.

"It depends on the crime," said Hamish. "Now if you'd poisoned your mother or..."

"No, nothing like that," said Alice. "Look, when I was about Charlie's age, I threw a brick through Mr. Jenkins' window for a dare. Mr. Jenkins was a nasty old man who lived in our street. The other girls egged me on. Well, he got me charged and taken to court. All I got was a warning and Mum had to pay for the window and the local paper put a couple of lines about it at the bottom of one of their pages. I mean, it was a silly little thing, really, but would a man like Jeremy mind? You see, he's awfully ambitious and...and...well, he plans to stand for Parliament, and...and...oh, do you know now I've told you, I realize I've been worrying about nothing. I should have told *him*. In fact, I'd better before anyone else does. How he'll laugh!"

"If it's that unimportant," said Hamish, pouring himself more tea, "then I am thinking that there is no need whateffer to tell anyone at all. In my opinion, Miss Wilson, Mr. Blythe is something of a snob and would not normally be interested in you were he not on holiday..."

Alice leapt to her feet. *"You're* the snob," she said. "And rude, too. I'll show you. I'll tell Jeremy right now and when I'm Mrs. Blythe, you can eat your words."

"As you please." Hamish shrugged. Alice rushed out of the house and slammed the kitchen door with a bang. Hamish cursed himself for being clumsy. Alice reminded him of Ann Grant, a young girl brought up in Lochdubh, only passably pretty. She had been seen around one of the flashier holiday guests two summers ago, driving with him everywhere in his car, and gossiping about the grand wedding she would have. But the holidaymaker had left and Ann had gone about ill and red-eyed. She had been packed off suddenly to a relative in Glasgow. The village gossips said she had gone to have an abortion and was now walking the streets. But Hamish had heard through *his* relatives that she was working as a typist in a Glasgow office and had said she never wanted to see Lochdubh or her family again. If her family hadn't been so common, she said, then her beau would have married her.

Snobbery is a terrible thing, thought Hamish dismally. It can almost kill young girls. Would they kill because of it? That was a question well worth turning over.

ALICE RAN ALL the way back to the hotel and straight up to Jeremy's room. She pounded on the door until a muffled voice shouted, "The door's open. I'm in the bathroom."

She pushed open the door. Perhaps the murder had made her a little crazy or perhaps Alice had lived in a fantasy world for too long, but she justified her next action by persuading herself that they were going to be married, or would be married if she established a basis of intimacy. She strolled casually into the bathroom and sat on the edge of the bath.

"Hello, darling," she said.

Jeremy hastily floated a large sponge over himself to act as a fig leaf and asked carefully, without looking at her, "Have you been drinking? I know we're all shattered by this murder business but..."

Alice came down to reality with a bump. "I'll wait for you in the bedroom," she gasped. "I've got something I *must* tell you."

She sat nervously on the bed by the window, fidgeting with the curtain cord and wishing she hadn't been so *bold*.

Jeremy came out with a white towel knotted around his waist and drying his hair with another.

Alice turned her face away and twisted a handkerchief nervously in her hands.

"*Now* you look like your usual self," said Jeremy. "For a moment there I thought you were going to rape me."

"Don't make fun of me," said Alice, wishing

he wouldn't look so amused, so *detached*. What if Macbeth should prove to be right?

But if they were married, it might come out. Better tell him now. And so Alice did, simply plunging into her story at the beginning and charging on until the end.

As she talked, she was back there in that dusty court on that hot summer's day with the tar melting on the roads outside. She could still remember her mother, crying with shame. She could remember her own sick feeling of disgrace.

When she finished, she looked at Jeremy awkwardly. He was studying her face in an intent, serious way. Jeremy was actually wondering whether to share his own guilty secret and at the same time noticing how Alice's schoolgirlish blouse was strained against her small, high breasts. God, it had been ages since... Then there was all this fear and worry about the murder. Yes, he knew why Alice had dreaded Lady Jane printing that bit of childhood nonsense. Hadn't he himself gone through hell to try to shut her mouth? He glanced at the clock. Eight-thirty. Too early for a drink but not too early for that other tranquillizer.

He sat down beside Alice on the bed and drew her against his still-damp body. "You don't mind?" whispered Alice.

"Of course not," he said, stroking her hair. She smelled of nervous sweat, sharp and acrid, mixed with lavender talcum powder. He put a hand on one little breast and began to stroke it.

Alice shivered against him. She was not a virgin, having lost that through curiosity and drink two years ago in the back of a car after a party with a man whose name she could not remember. It had been a painful and degrading experience, but he had been a heavy, vulgar sort of man.

Women's Lib has a long way to go before it gets *inside* girls like Alice. As his lips began to move against her own, her one thought was, "If I sleep with him, he'll have to marry me."

As they lay stretched out on the bed, pressed together, as Alice's clothes were removed, she had an idiotic wish that Jeremy might have been wearing some sort of status symbol, his gold wrist watch, say. For when the all-too-brief foreplay was over and she was rammed into the bed by the panting, struggling weight of this man, it all seemed as painful and degrading as that time in the back of the car. She wished he'd hurry up and get it over with. There was that terrible tyranny of the orgasm. What *was* it? He was obviously waiting for something to happen to her. She had read about women shrieking in ecstasy, but if she shrieked, she might bring people rushing in, thinking there had been another murder.

His silence was punctuated by grunts, not words of love. At last, just when she thought she could not bear it any longer, he collapsed on top of her. She let out a long sigh of relief, and Jeremy kissed her ear and said, "It was good for you too," mistaking her sigh for one of satisfaction.

"I love you, Jeremy," whispered Alice, winding her arms around him and hugging that vision of sports car, expensive clothes, good accent, and Member of Parliament.

"Do you?" He propped himself up on one elbow. "That's nice." He kissed her nose and then smacked her on the bottom. "Better get dressed. Gosh, I'm hungry."

Alice scooped up her clothes and scuttled into the bathroom. After she had showered and dressed, she felt better. Love in the morning. How sophisticated. How deliciously decadent.

She was just putting on lipstick when Jeremy shouted through the door, "I'll see you in the dining room. Don't be long."

Alice's hand jerked nervously, and she smeared lipstick over her cheek. She scrubbed it off with a tissue and then ran out, hoping to catch him, but he had already left.

When she went out into the corridor, two maids were stuffing dirty sheets into a hamper and they looked at her curiously. "Good morning," said Alice, staring at both of them hard as if challenging them to voice their evil thoughts.

The fishing party was grouped around one large table in the far corner as if the management had decided to put them in quarantine. The Roths were there and Daphne, the major and Jeremy. Charlie would be having breakfast with his aunt, but where were the Cartwrights?

"Don't know," shrugged Daphne. "I think they jolly well ought to be here handing out refunds. Pass the marmalade, Jeremy darling."

Alice frowned. It was time to stake her claim. She slid into a chair beside Jeremy and took his hand under the table, gave it a squeeze, and smiled at him in an intimate way.

"I need both hands to eat, Alice," said Jeremy crossly. Alice snatched her hand away and Daphne giggled.

HEATHER AND JOHN Cartwright were sitting in Hamish's cluttered kitchen, eating bacon baps and drinking tea. They had explained they were "just passing."

It was Heather who had had the impulse to talk

to Hamish. Hamish was a good sounding board because he *was* the law, and although he could hardly be described as a strong arm of it, he was in a position to overhear how the investigation was proceeding.

"I just hope this won't break the fishing school," said John gloomily.

"I should not think so," said Hamish, turning bacon deftly in the pan. "Provided, of course, the murderer is found. It will be in the way of being an added attraction."

"I was shocked when Blair told me she was really that awful columnist woman."

Hamish stood very still, his back to them as he worked at the stove. "And you did not know this before?" he asked.

There was a little silence, and then John said, "Of course not. Had we known then we should not have allowed her to come."

"Aye, but did you not know after she had arrived?" asked Hamish.

Again that silence. Hamish turned round, the bacon slice in one hand.

"No, we did not," said Heather emphatically.

Hamish carefully and slowly lifted the bacon from the pan and put it on a plate. He turned off the gas. He lifted his cup of tea from beside the

stove and came and joined Heather and John at the
table.

"I happen to know that you had a letter from
Austria. You see, you threw it out of the window, hoping it would land in the loch. The tide
was out and the boy Charlie picked it up because
the stamp attracted his attention. I would not normally read anyone else's mail, but when it comes to
murder, well, I don't have that many fine scruples.
It was from a couple of friends of yours in Austria who ran a ski resort until Lady Jane came on
holiday."

"You have no right to read private mail," shouted
John.

Hamish looked at him stolidly.

Heather put a hand on John's arm. "It's no use,"
she said wearily. "We did know. We were frightened. This school is our life. Years of hard work
have gone into building it up. We thought she was
going to take it away from us."

"But the couple at the ski resort turned out to be
married to other people, not each other," pointed
out Hamish. "They said the publicity by Lady Jane
ruined them only because Mr. Bergen, the ski resort
owner, had not been paying alimony for years. You
are surely both not in that sort of position. When
you found out, would it not have been better to try

to tell the school, openly and in front of her, what she did for a living?"

"I didn't think of that," said John wretchedly. "You may as well know that I saw Jane on the night she was murdered. I went up to her room after dinner."

"And...?"

"And she just laughed at me. She said this sort of fly fishing in these waters was like grouse shooting or deer stalking—a sport for the rich. She said she was about to prove that the sort of people who went on these holidays were social climbers who deserved to be cut down to size."

"Deary me," said Hamish, stirring his tea, "was she a Communist?"

"I don't think she was a member of the Communist Party, if that's what you mean," said John. "She seemed to want to make people writhe. She was like a blackmailer who enjoys power. In Scotland they would say she was just agin everything."

"Did she say she was out to ruin the fishing school?"

"Not in so many words. But that's what she was setting out to do."

"What exactly did you say?"

"I said that I had worked hard to build up this school and I begged her not to harm it. She laughed at me and told me to get out. I said...I said..."

"Yes?" prompted Hamish gently.

"You'd better tell him," said Heather.

"I told her I would kill her," whispered John. "I shouted it. I'll have to tell Blair—I think Jeremy heard me."

"Mr. Blythe? Why would he hear you? Is his room next to hers?"

"No, he was out in the corridor when I left."

"What will we do, Mr. Macbeth?" pleaded Heather.

"I think you should tell Mr. Blair. If there's one thing that makes a detective like Blair suspicious, or any detective for that matter, it's finding out some-one's been hiding something. The pair of you have got nothing awful in your past that Lady Jane was about to expose?"

Both shook their heads.

"And apart from the short time that Mr. Cart-wright was with Lady Jane, you were together all night?"

"Why do you ask?" Heather had turned white.

"I ask," said Hamish patiently, "because any cop-per with a nasty mind might think that *one* of you might have sneaked off and bumped her off, if not the pair of you."

"We had better go," said Heather. "Tell Mr. Blair we're taking the class up to the Marag to fish. It's near enough. We must go on as if nothing had happened."

After they left, Hamish, who had already heard the sound of voices from his office at the front, ambled through with a cup of tea in one hand.

"Shouldn't you be in uniform?" growled Blair, who was seated behind Hamish's desk flanked by his two detectives.

"In a minute," said Hamish easily.

"And I told you to keep out of this. That was the Cartwrights I saw leaving."

"Aye."

"Well, what did they have to say for themselves?"

"Only that they knew something they hadn't told you and now thought they should. Also that they were taking the class up to the Marag which is quite close so that you can go and see any of the members quite easily."

"For Jesus buggering Christ's sake, don't they know this is a murder investigation?"

"Find any clues?" asked Hamish.

"Just one thing. If it had been like today, we might have found more traces. But most of the ground was baked hard. The procurator fiscal's report says she was strangled somewhere else and dragged along through the bushes and then thrown in the pool."

"And what is this clue?"

"It's just a bit of a photograph," said MacNab, before Blair could stop him. "Just a bit torn off the top corner. See."

He held out the bit of black and white photograph on a pair of tweezers. Hamish took it gingerly.

It showed the very top of a woman's head, or what he could only guess to be a woman's head because it had some sort of sparkly ornament on top like the edge of a tiara. Behind was a poster with the part legend BUY BRIT—.

"That might have been Buy British," said Hamish, "which means it would have been taken in the sixties when Wilson was running that Buy British campaign and that would therefore eliminate the younger members of the fish . . ."

"Listen to the great detective," jeered Blair. "We all reached that conclusion in two seconds flat. Why don't you trot off and find out if anyone's been raiding the poor box in one of those churches. Damn ridiculous having so many churches in a wee place like this."

Hamish turned to amble out. "And get your uniform on," shouted Blair.

"Now," said Blair, rustling through sheafs of statements. "According to these, they're all innocent. But one of them was so afraid that Lady Jane would print something about them that they killed her. So chase up all these people we phoned yesterday and hurry them up. And that includes background on the Roths. See if there's been a telex from the FBI. Find out if any of them have been in trouble with the police, although I think you'll have to dig deeper than that."

Hamish changed into his uniform, admitting to his reflection in the glass that he, Hamish Macbeth, was a very angry man. In fact, he could not quite remember being so angry in all his easygoing life. He was determined to go on talking to the members of the fishing school until someone said something that gave himself away. He was not going to be frightened because it was a murder investigation. All criminals were the same whether it was a theft in the school or poaching deer on the hills. You talked, asked questions, and listened and watched and waited. The hell with Blair. He would go up to the Marag and find out what Jeremy had been doing outside Lady Jane's room. As he left by the back door, the press were entering the police station by the front. At least Lochdubh would be spared their headlines until the following morning. The newspapers were always a day late.

In any common-or-garden murder, the press would not hang about longer than a day or two. But this murderee had a title and the location was well away from their office with out-of-town expenses, so they would all try to spin it out as long as they could. Of course, Lady Jane had been one of their own, so to speak, and Hamish had learned from his relative in Fleet Street some time ago that the press were not like the police: they were notoriously uninterested in anything that happened to one of their ranks except as a subject for gossip.

The day was warm and sweaty, and although the rain had stopped, there was a thick mist everywhere and the midges were out in clouds. Hamish took a stick of repellent out of his tunic pocket and rubbed his face and neck with it.

When he reached the Marag, it was to find the fishing school diligently at work, looking like some old army-jungle movie, as each one had a mosquito net shrouding the face.

Hamish scanned the anonymous figures, picked out Heather and John by virtue of their expert casting rather than their appearance, and Charlie because of his size and because his mother was sitting on a rock nearby, flapping away the mosquitoes and watching her son as if expecting him to be dragged off to prison at any moment. Hamish went to join her.

"I think this is ridiculous," she burst out as soon

as she saw him. "It's horrible weather and the whole school should be broken up and sent home."

"They seem quite happy," said Hamish.

"I don't understand it," wailed Mrs. Baxter. "Those Cartwrights suggested the school should try to go on as if nothing has happened, and they all leapt at it when just a moment before they had been threatening to ask for their money back. I told my Charlie *he* was coming straight home with me, and he *defied* me. Just like his father." Two large tears of self-pity formed in Mrs. Baxter's eyes and she dabbed at them furiously with a tissue. "I knew I should never have let Charlie come all the way up here. The minute I got his letter, I was on the train."

"Aye, and when did you arrive?"

"I *told* the police. I got to Lochdubh just after the terrible murder."

"Then how is it that Mrs. MacPherson down at the bakery saw you the night before?"

"It wasn't me. It must have been someone else."

"Blair will check the buses and so on, you know," said Hamish. "It's always better to tell the truth. If you don't, it looks as if you might have something to hide. Did you know Lady Jane was a newspaperwoman?"

Mrs. Baxter sat in silence, twisting the damp tissue in her fingers. Rain dripped from her southwester.

"She's been around the neighbourhood asking questions," said Mrs. Baxter at last in a low voice. "I've never got on with my neighbours and I know they told her all about the divorce. But what's divorce? Half the population of Britain get divorced every year. I've nothing to be ashamed of and that I told her."

"You *told* Lady Jane?"

"Well, I phoned her before I got on the train," said Mrs. Baxter miserably, "and I said if she wrote anything about my Charlie I would..."

"Kill her?"

"People say all sorts of things they don't mean when they're angry," said Mrs. Baxter defiantly. "This is a wretched business. Do you know that detective, MacNab, was round at the house last night asking for Charlie's leader?"

"No, I did not. I'm shocked."

"So you should be. Suspecting a mere child."

"It is not that that shocks me but the fact that they did not immediately check all the leaders earlier in the day. Was anyone's leader missing?"

"*I* don't know. *You* should know. They fingerprinted everyone as well."

Out of the corner of his eye, Hamish saw a white police car moving slowly round the edge of the loch. He moved quickly out of sight behind a stand of trees and made his way silently along a rabbit track that led back down to the village. Jeremy would have to wait. Hamish went straight to the hotel and asked the manager, Mr. Johnson, where the press had disappeared to, since he would have expected them to be up at the loch, photographing the school.

"There's a big Jack the Ripper sort of murder broken in London," said Mr. Johnson, "and that's sent most of them scampering back home. The nationals anyway. This is small beer by comparison. Also, Blair got the water bailiffs to block the private road to the Marag. He hates the press. Going to solve the murder for us, Mr. Macbeth?"

"Aye, maybe." Hamish grinned. "Any hope of a wee shufty at Lady Jane's room?"

"Blair had it locked, of course. No one's to go in. Police commandment."

"I'm the police, so there'll be no harm in letting me in."

"I suppose. Come along then. But I think you'd better try to leave things as they are. I've a feeling that Blair doesn't like you."

Hamish followed the manager upstairs and along the corridors of the hotel. "They took a plan of all the hotel rooms," said Mr. Johnson over his shoulder. "I don't know what they expect to learn from that because it's said she was strangled up on the hillside in the middle of the night, not far from where she was shoved in the pool. They've found a bittie of a photograph, and Blair got everybody down to the last chambermaid fingerprinted. No fingerprints on the photo, of course, and none on those chains that were around her legs, as if there would be anything worthwhile after that time of churning and bashing about that pool. But Mr. Blair likes to throw his weight around. Here we are."

He put the key in the lock and opened the door. Lady Jane had occupied a suite with a good view of the loch. "I'll leave you to it," said Mr. Johnson cheerfully. "I can't feel sad about this murder. It's turned out good for business. Every lunch and dinner is booked up solid for the next few weeks. They're coming from as far as Aberdeen, but then these oil people have more money than sense."

Left alone, Hamish stood in the middle of the bedroom and looked around. Surely it must have dawned on Blair before anything else that Lady Jane would have brought notes of some kind. Yes, of course it had. Fingerprint dust lay like grey snow on every surface. Well, they would hardly come back for *more* fingerprints. Hamish began his search. The suite consisted of a small entrance hall with a side table and one chair, a tiny sitting room with a writing desk, television set and two easy chairs, and a bedroom with a bathroom leading off it.

There was a typewriter open on the writing desk with a pile of hotel writing paper beside it. He diligently searched the top of the desk and drawers. There was not a single piece of paper with any writing on it whatsoever. Perhaps Blair had taken away what there was.

He turned his attention to the bedroom. He slid open drawers of frivolous underwear—Lady Jane's taste in that direction was rather startling—and rummaged underneath. Nothing. If she had had a handbag, then Blair must have taken it away. Two suitcases lay on a luggage rack at the foot of the bed. Locked.

He took a large ring of keys out of his tunic pocket and got to work, listening all the while in case Blair should choose that moment to return for another search. At last the first case sprang open. There was a lavender sachet, two detective stories, a box of heated rollers, and a hair dryer. No paper of any kind. The next suitcase was completely empty.

He looked under the bed, under the mattress, down the sides of the chairs, even in the toilet tank and the bathroom cupboard, but not one scrap of paper did he find.

The manager had left the keys in the door.

Hamish carefully locked the room and deposited the keys in the manager's office.

He decided to go back to the Marag to see if the field was clear. But as he was making his way out of the hotel, he heard voices from the interviewing room and noticed Alice sitting nervously in the lounge outside.

"He's got Jeremy in there," said Alice. "Will this never end? He's going to see me next and then call in the others one by one. I told Jeremy about that court thing and he didn't mind, so you were wrong."

"Is that a fact?" said Hamish, looking down at her curiously.

Alice jerked her head to one side to avoid the policeman's gaze. Jeremy had been offhand all day, to say the least.

Hamish left quickly, deciding to try to find out a bit about the background of the others. He had in his tunic a list of the names and addresses of the members of the school. Perhaps he should start by trying to find out something about the Roths. But he could not use the telephone at the police station because Blair had set up headquarters there, and although he was busy interviewing Jeremy, no doubt his team of officers would be in the office.

Hamish's car was parked outside his house. He

decided to take a run up to the Halburton-Smythes.
The rain had stopped falling and a light breeze had
sprung up. But everything was wet and sodden and
grey. Mist shrouded the mountains, and wet, long-
haired sheep scampered across the road in front of
the car on their spindly black legs like startled fur-
coated schoolmarms.

He swung off the main road and up the narrower
one which led through acres of grouse moor to the
Halburton-Smythes' home. Home was a mock castle, built by a beer baron in the nineteenth century
when Queen Victoria made the Highlands fashionable. It had pinnacles, turrets and battlements and a
multitude of small, cold, dark rooms.

Hamish pushed open the massive, brass-studded
front door and walked into the stone-flagged gloom
of the hall. He made his way through to the estate
office, expecting to find Mr. Halburton-Smythe's
secretary, Lucy Hanson, there, but the room was
deserted and the bright red telephone sitting on the
polished mahogany desk seemed to beg Hamish to
reach out and use it.

He sat down beside the desk and after some
thought phoned Rory Grant at the *Daily Recorder*
in Fleet Street. Rory sounded exasperated when
he came on the line. "What's the use of having a
bobby for a relative if I can't get an exclusive on a

nice juicy murder? I had my bags packed and was going to set out on the road north when the Libyans decided to put a bomb in Selfridges and some Jack the Ripper started cutting up brass nails in Brixton, so I'm kept here. No one cares about your bloody murder now, but you might have given me a buzz. I called the police station several times, and some copper told me each time to piss off."

"It would still be news if I found the murderer, Rory," cajoled Hamish. "You know the people who are at the fishing school. The names have been in all the papers. See if you can find out a bit more about them than has appeared. Oh, and while I'm on the phone, if I wanted to find out about someone from New York who might have been in trouble, or someone from Augusta, Georgia, what would I do?"

"You phone the FBI, don't you, you great Highland berk."

"I think Detective Chief Inspector Blair will have done that and I would not want to go treading on any toes."

"You can phone the newspapers, then, but you'll need to wait until I go and get names from the foreign desk. You are a pest, Hamish."

Hamish held the line patiently until Rory returned with the information.

He thanked the reporter and, after listening to

the silence of the castle for a few moments, dialled New York. He was in luck. The reporter Rory had recommended said cheerfully it was a slack day and did Hamish want him to call back. "No, I will chust wait," said Hamish, comfortably aware that he was not paying for the call.

After some time the reporter came back with the information on Marvin Roth. "All old history," he said cheerfully. "Seems that back around 1970, he was in trouble over running sweatshops in the garment district. Employing illegal aliens and paying them peanuts. Big stink. Never got to trial. Bribed his way out of it. Wants to go into politics. Big man in town now. Donates to charities, fashionable pinko, ban the bomb and clean up the environment. No one's going to rake up his past. Got a nasty way of hitting back. Knows all the big names and he's a buddy of my editor's, so don't say where you got the information from, for Chrissake."

"Do you mean to tell me that you cannot print the facts?"

"Absolutely."

"It is all very strange," said Hamish, shaking his head. "I have never been to New York. What is the weather like at the moment?"

They chatted amiably for five more minutes at Mr. Halburton-Smythe's expense before Hamish remembered the BUY BRIT—on the section of photograph. It seemed that it must be Buy British, but could it perhaps be an American advertisement?

"Never heard of anything like it," said the American reporter cheerfully, "but I'll ask around." Hamish gave him the Halburton-Smythes' phone number and told the reporter to give any information to Priscilla.

Then he phoned Augusta, Georgia. Here he was unlucky. The reporter sounded cross and harried. No, he didn't know anything about Amy Roth, née Blanchard, off the top of his head. Yes, he would phone back, but he couldn't promise.

Hamish put down the telephone and sighed.

He heard the sound of heavy footsteps in the corridor and jumped to his feet. Colonel Halburton-Smythe erupted into the room. He was a small, thin, choleric man in his late fifties. Hamish marvelled anew that the fair Priscilla could have such an awful father.

"What are you doing here, Officer?" barked the colonel, looking suspiciously at the phone.

"I was waiting for your good self," said Hamish. "Miss Halburton-Smythe told me you were still having trouble with the poachers."

"I've just been down to your wretched station.

Fat chappie told me he was in the middle of a murder investigation. Told him one of my deer had been shot in the leg last night. Gave me a wall-eyed stare. Useless, the lot of you. What are you going to do about it?"

"I will look into the matter," said Hamish soothingly.

"See that you do, and while we're on the subject of poaching, I believe you've been squiring my daughter to the local flea pit. It's got to stop."

"It was not a den of vice," said Hamish patiently. "And I would say Miss Halburton-Smythe is old enough to know her own mind."

"If I find you sniffing around my daughter again," said the colonel rudely, "I'll report you to your superiors."

"You should not let yourself be getting in the bad temper," said Hamish soothingly. "Why, I can see the wee red veins breaking out all over your eyeballs. A terrible thing is the high blood pressure. Why, I mind . . ."

"Get out!"

"Very well." Hamish sauntered off with maddening slowness.

Once out in the drive, however, he could not resist loitering and looking around for a glimpse of Priscilla.

"If you think you're going to see my daughter," barked the colonel behind him, "have another think. She's gone out for the day with John Harrington, Lord Harrington's son, and for your further information, she is shortly going to become engaged to him."

Hamish realized with some amazement that hearts actually did ache. Without replying, he walked to his car, climbed in and, without once looking at the colonel again, he drove off.

When he arrived at the police station, it was to find Blair and MacNab were still at the hotel and the suspicious-eyed detective, Jimmy Anderson, was sitting behind the desk in the office.

Hamish noticed a woman's handbag on the desk. "Would that be Lady Jane's?" he asked.

"Yes," grunted the detective without looking up.

"And would she maybe have a diary or anything with notes?"

"No, she did not," said Jimmy Anderson. "Deil a piece o' paper or a note. Her money's there and her credit cards and cheque-book."

"And it was in her room?"

"Aye, and Mr. Blair still thinks someone killed her to stop her publishing something."

"What have you got on them, just by way of a wee gossip?" Hamish reached a hand into a vase and produced a bottle of Scotch. "You'll be having a dram, of course."

"That's very kind of you," said Anderson, visibly thawing. "Don't see any harm in telling you, only don't tell Blair. Cheers. Right, now. We're waiting to hear about the Roths. Blair's keen on them all of a sudden despite that Buy British thing. He thinks there's a chance Roth might have Mafia connections and Lady Jane might have been on to it. Would damage his career."

"Would it now," said Hamish, pouring himself a whisky. "Mind you, it doesn't seem to have got in the way of an American politician's career before. What about Amy Roth?"

"We're trying to find a bit on her too."

"But Lady Jane would not have had the time to find out about the Roths. I mean, if it's that difficult."

"All these bookings were made at least eight months ago and that's when Lady Jane got the list. She's been in the States since then."

"She certainly worked hard for her living," said Hamish. "A little more to warm you, Mr. Anderson?"

"Thank you. Call me Jimmy. As to the rest, Jeremy Blythe's got an interest in politics as well. He was supposed to be sent down from Oxford for having an affair with the wife of one of the dons, but there's more to it than that. While he was having an affair with her, he also found time to get one of the local barmaids pregnant, and her husband raised a stink at the college. That way the don's wife found out and made a stink. Then he owed money all over the place although Daddy's rich. Wasn't studying. Sent down and finished his degree at London University. Became respectable but is still paying for the upkeep of the barmaid's kid. Her husband settled for that out of court. Daddy bought him a partnership, but he's been making rumblings of becoming the next Conservative candidate. At a party last year, old friend from Oxford started ribbing him about the barmaid and this Jeremy punched him rotten. Police called in but no charges. Filthy temper, he has.

"Alice Wilson chucked a brick through a neighbour's window when she was a kid and ended up in court. Not much there.

"Daphne Gore comes from a rich family. Caused a scandal by running off with a Spanish waiter who, it turned out, had no intention of marrying her but had to be bought off by Daphne's parents. Girl went into a depression and was in a psychiatric clinic for a few months. Could be a bit of insanity still around.

"Heather and John Cartwright. Very suspicious. Owned up they knew Lady Jane was out to get the school and they're both fishing mad. Not a sport with *them*, more a religion.

"Charlie Baxter. You can never tell with kids of that age, but I'm sure he's out of it. The mother, on the other hand, is an hysterical type."

"And the major?" prompted Hamish. "He was more humiliated by Lady Jane than any of them."

"Oh, the fishing and all that. We heard about how he'd threatened to kill her. Don't think there's anything to worry about there. Fine old soldier. Blair likes him. But we're waiting for a full report."

There was the crunch of wheels on the gravel outside. One minute Hamish was lounging in the chair opposite Anderson. The next he was gone—and the bottle of whisky.

Hamish ambled along the front. A pale sun was beginning to turn the mist to gold, and there was a long patch of greenish-blue sky out on the horizon where the tiny white dot of a yacht bucketed about to show the approaching wind beyond the shelter of the harbour. The tide was out, leaving an expanse of oily pebbled beach scattered with the debris of storms and flotsam and jetsam from boats.

He tried to focus his whole mind on the problem of the murder to banish the haunting picture of Priscilla languishing away the afternoon in this man Harrington's arms.

Then he saw the Roths approaching. They were an odd pair, he thought. Amy was a big, soft woman, but Marvin's six feet topped her by a few inches. Although her movements were usually slow and calm, there seemed an underlying restlessness about her. She was wearing a trouser suit of faded denim with a scarf knotted about her throat. Marvin had changed into his usual sombre black business suit, and his bald head shone in the yellow light from the sea.

"When is all this going to end?" demanded Marvin as the couple came abreast of Hamish. "Amy isn't used to being treated the way she's been by your coppers. That Blair thinks he's hot shit."

"I'm used to being treated like a lady," said Amy. "I thought all you Britishers were supposed to be gentlemen."

"We're just like other folk," said Hamish soothingly. "Like sweeties. We come in all shapes and sizes and some of us are horrible."

"Sweeties?" queried Amy, momentarily diverted.

"Candy," translated Marvin. "See here, Amy's like aristocracy back home. This Blair wouldn't treat your Queen like this."

"It's to my way of thinking that he might," said Hamish.

"Well, it's a pity Amy's folks have all passed

away or they would have something to say about this."

Hamish looked at Amy as Marvin spoke and noticed the tightening of the skin at the corners of her eyelids and the way she was obviously ferreting around in her mind for a change of subject. He had a sudden intuition that Amy had been lying about her background. Well, a lot of people did, but they didn't go around committing murder when they were found out. Or did they?

"Why doesn't Blair just arrest that major? He's the only one who had it in for Lady Jane," said Amy. "You heard about his trick with the salmon?"

"Oh, aye, the gossip went two times around the village and back again. It is very hard to keep anything quiet in the Highlands."

Amy muttered something like, "Just like red hook," and Hamish wondered whether it was something to do with fishing.

"Except murder," said Marvin. "This place is the asshole of the world. I don't like the country, I don't like the hick servants at the hotel. What's a FEB?"

"Nothing that would apply to you, Mr. Roth. It is just an expression the barman uses."

"Him!" said Marvin with great contempt. "He can't even make a dry martini. One part gin to three parts warm French is his idea. Jeez, the fuckers in this dump piss me off."

"Honey," pleaded Amy, "watch your language."

Hamish's red eyebrows had vanished up under his cap with shock.

"Sorry," said Marvin wearily. "I guess I'm frightened. I feel trapped here. If we're going for this goddam constitutional, then we'd better get on with it."

"Catch any fish?" asked Hamish.

"Jeremy and Heather caught a trout each," said Marvin, "but those salmon just can't be caught, in my opinion. They just jump about the place and keep well away from the hooks."

"I could lend you one of my flies," volunteered Hamish. "I have had a bit of luck with it."

"Say, why don't you join us for dinner tonight and bring it with you," said Marvin. "Everyone knows you're not on the case and we're getting a bit sick of each other. After all, one of us did it and we all sit around wondering who's going to be next."

Hamish accepted the invitation and went on his way.

As he approached the hotel, he saw Jeremy coming down towards it from the direction of the Marag, still wearing his fishing gear.

"Got one!" he shouted as Hamish approached. He held up a fair-sized trout.

"Let's get into the hotel," said Hamish, noticing a reporter and photographer heading in their direction.

They walked together into the little room where Jeremy placed his catch on the scales and logged the weight in the book. "I was hearing that you were seen in the corridor outside Lady June's room the night she was murdered," said Hamish.

"Nonsense," said Jeremy, carefully lifting his fish off the scales. "Aren't you supposed to be out of this investigation? I don't think Blair would like to hear you had been asking questions."

"Maybe not. But he would like to hear what you'd been up to," said Hamish.

"Then tell him and much good it may do you," yelled Jeremy. He rushed off, nearly bumping into Alice, who was watching them anxiously. Alice ran after Jeremy and, undeterred by the fact that he had slammed his room door in her face, she opened it and went in. He was sitting hunched on the edge of the bed. "That blasted, nosy copper," he said without looking up.

Alice sat down beside him and took his hand in hers. "What's the matter, Jeremy?" she pleaded. "You've been awful to me all day."

"Christ, I've got enough on my mind without worrying about you," snapped Jeremy. "I was seen outside Lady Jane's room on the night of the murder."

"Oh, Jeremy. What happened?"

"My father phoned me and told me about her. I got into a silly mess when I was at Oxford and I wanted to make sure she kept her mouth shut. She said if I spent the night with her, she would think about it. Can you imagine? That awful old cow."

Alice tried to withdraw her hand. What if Jeremy had murdered Lady Jane? He looked so odd, older, grimmer, and there was a muscle jumping in his left cheek.

Jeremy turned and looked at her. "It wouldn't have mattered so much if she had written about you," said Alice timidly. "I mean, it wasn't so very bad."

"You don't know anything about it," snapped Jeremy. In a flat voice, he told Alice of his Oxford scandals, although he omitted the fact he was still paying for the support of the barmaid's child.

"I could never have gone in for politics," he said. He felt shaken with nerves and anger. How stupid he'd been not to have told Hamish the whole thing. He needed a drink...or something.

He seized Alice suddenly and pulled her down on the bed. "Oh, Jeremy," whispered Alice, forgetting that she had thought him a murderer a moment ago, "do you love me?"

"Yes, yes," mumbled Jeremy against her hair. He started to unbutton her blouse, and Alice was so thrilled and excited that he had confessed his love that she almost enjoyed the next ten minutes.

Day Six

Hope not for minde in women.

—John Donne

Hamish was up very early. He had been unable to sleep. It had been a miserable dinner party. Only Alice had seemed to enjoy herself. Daphne Gore appeared to be haunted by the spirit of Lady Jane in that she had seemed hell-bent on ruining the evening for everyone. Hamish could only be glad young Charlie was not present. The boy was suffering enough from hysterical women in the shape of his mother. Hamish had worn the dark grey suit that he kept for his occasional visits to church, and Daphne Gore had said he looked dressed for a funeral. She had then started to harangue the Roths over the American Cruise missiles, although it was evident to all that she was merely trying to be bitchy and didn't care much one way or the other.

They had all drunk too much, because Amy had the nervous habit of constantly refilling their glasses without waiting for the waiter to come around.

And then as the climax to a truly horrible evening, Priscilla had arrived for dinner at the hotel with John Harrington. Harrington was everything Hamish detested in a man. He had a loud, carrying English voice, he fussed over the wine, he criticized the food. He had beautifully tailored clothes, a square, immaculately barbered chin, a tanned rugged face, and crinkly brown hair. And he made Priscilla laugh.

Hamish decided to take his boat out and try to catch some mackerel. He wandered down to the beach and untied the painter of his rowing boat. It was then that he saw the small figure of Charlie Baxter wistfully watching him.

"Want to go out with me?" called Hamish, and Charlie scampered down the beach.

"What are you doing out so early, laddie?" asked Hamish. "It isn't even six o'clock yet."

"I wanted to get out," said Charlie. "My mother won't mind. I often go out early for a walk. Things are pretty rough. I want to stay on with Auntie, and Mother wants me to go back."

"Maybe I'll have a wee word with her," said Hamish. "Hop in and keep still."

Charlie obeyed, sitting in the boat while Hamish pushed it out into the still waters of Lochdubh. The sun was just peeping over the horizon. The water was like glass, and the sky above was cloudless. "Looks as if it's going to be a hot day," said Hamish, climbing in and taking the oars. He rowed them steadily out into the loch.

"Where are we going?" asked Charlie.

"To catch mackerel. Dead easy."

"What with?"

"A spinner. I'll stop in a bit and show you how to do it."

"Are we going right out to sea?"

"No, just a bit further."

Charlie relapsed into silence, hanging over the side of the boat and staring at the sunlight dancing on the water.

Hamish at last shipped the oars and picked up a reel of stout twine with several hooks and silver spinners attached to it.

"Do we bait the hooks?" asked Charlie with interest.

"No, the spinners do the trick. Mackerel will go for nearly anything. That's why they're sometimes called the scavengers of the sea. Just unwind the line and let it trail out behind the boat," said Hamish.

He began to row again, this time slowly and easily, shipping the oars from time to time.

Behind them, smoke began to rise from the chimneys of the village, and the twisted grotesque forms of the mountains stood out sharp against the clear sky.

"Stop the boat," shrieked Charlie suddenly. "I think there's something biting."

"Pull in the line," said Hamish, shipping the oars. Charlie wound the line in feverishly. "There's fish on the end," he said. "Fish!"

"Pull them in, there's a good lad."

Charlie jerked the line and hooks, spinners, fish and all crashed behind him in the boat.

"There's four mackerel," said Charlie as Hamish expertly dislodged the hooks and killed the fish. "Can we try again?"

"Och, no," said Hamish. "We'll just keep to what we can eat. Ready for breakfast?"

"You mean we'll *cook* them?"

"Of course we will. It's too early to wake your mother, so we'll drop a note through the door to tell her where you are."

Looking more childlike than Hamish had seen him before, Charlie smiled shyly and said, "You know, everything's really so much better now that terrible woman has gone. I wish I could stay here."

"But your auntie has just come up for the summer."

"I overheard her say that she would stay on and put me to the school in Strathbane if my mother would leave me."

"And you would like that?"

"Yes, Mr. Macbeth. There's that Mr. Blair waiting for you on the beach," said Charlie. "Does that mean we can't cook our catch?"

"No, whatever happens, we'll have time to eat."

But Hamish privately thought it must be something very important to get Mr. Blair out of his bed so early.

"Well, we've got our man," said Mr. Blair after Hamish had pulled up his boat on the beach. "While you were out enjoying yourself and playing with the weans, I got a call from Scotland Yard. Major Peter Frame was arrested two years ago for trying to strangle the secretary of the Buffers Club in Pall Mall. What d'you make of that?"

"I would say it was still not proof the man strangled Lady Jane."

"Yes, well that's why you're a village bobby and I'm not. The man threatened her in front of witnesses."

"Have you arrested him?"

"Not yet. He's just helping us with our inquiries."

"I gather he's got a fine war record."

"Not him," sneered Blair. "That's something else we found out about him. He looks old enough, God knows, but he's only fifty-four. He never was in the war, he never saw any action. He was a major in the Educational Corps in some unit down in Lincolnshire."

"I am sure Lady Jane knew that," said Hamish slowly.

"We're managing fine without your help, although instead of wasting your time fishing, you might see to your duties. That prick, Halburton-Smythe, was howling down the phone last night about some poacher."

"I will see to it," said Hamish, but Blair was already striding away.

Hamish stood looking after the detective, lost in thought. What if there had been a Lady Jane present at one of the other fishing classes? Would the same lies and petty snobberies have risen to the surface as well?

Charlie tugged his sleeve. "I rather like Major Frame," he said. "He's a bit of an ass, but he's jolly kind."

"Let's leave a note for your mother," said Hamish, "and then we will have our breakfast."

But before he cooked breakfast, he phoned Angus

MacGregor, a layabout who lived on the other side of the village.

"Is that yourself?" said Hamish. "Aye, well, Angus, your sins have found you out because I am coming to arrest you after I have had my breakfast."

Charlie listened with interest as the phone squawked.

"Nonsense," said Hamish at last. "Havers. You bought that new rifle and it is well known that you could not hit the barn door. I will be over soon with the handcuffs."

Hamish put the phone down and grinned at Charlie.

"If he knows you are going to arrest him he might run away," said the boy, round-eyed.

"That's just what he will do," said Hamish, leading the way to the kitchen. "We'd best hide out in here, for they'll be along with the major any moment. Yes, you see Angus has the wife and three children and it would not be right to take their useless father away from them to prison, so he will probably go to Aberdeen for a bit and he will return when he thinks I have forgotten about it. But he will not be trying to bag one of the colonel's stags again."

After a sustaining breakfast of mackerel dipped in oatmeal and fried in butter, Hamish accompanied

Charlie home and was shortly closeted with Mrs. Baxter for what seemed to the anxiously awaiting Charlie a very long time indeed.

When he emerged, he merely ruffled Charlie's curls and took himself off.

He wandered along to the hotel to learn what the fishing school intended to do for the day. He found them all, with the exception of young Charlie and the major, seated in the lounge, getting a lecture on the ways of trout and salmon from John.

The Roths, Daphne, Jeremy and Alice were in high spirits. Even John Cartwright was cracking jokes. All had heard of the major's "arrest," and all were determined to believe him guilty.

"It seems as if Mr. Blair won't be needing to grill us anymore," said John, "so we can go back to Loch Alsh and get some good fishing."

As they all left the hotel, Hamish noticed that Jeremy had an arm around Alice's shoulders.

Alice had spent the whole night in Jeremy's bed. She felt light-headed with debility, happiness and relief. It was awful to have to go to the Cartwrights' estate car with Charlie who had just joined the party and leave Jeremy with Daphne, but he had promised to spend the day with her, Alice, and now she was sure he was on the point of proposing.

The nightmare was over. The murderer had

been arrested. Alice, like the rest, had not really believed that "helping the police with their inquiries" stuff. She began to wonder if she would have to give evidence at the trial. That would be exciting since she no longer had anything to fear from the newspapers.

The countryside now looked friendly. Heather blazed purple down the flanks of the mountain sides, and a peregrine falcon soared high in the wind currents in the sky above.

And then a little cloud began to appear on the sunny horizon of Alice's mind. The clean, clear air was invigorating. Set against it, the dark, blanket-tussled writhings of the previous night seemed grimy. Then, again, he had not waited for her but had rushed off for breakfast, leaving her to make her own way down. There had been no long days of exchanged glances and holding hands. Alice shrugged and tried to feel worldly-wise. Wham bang, thank you, ma'am, was reality. All men were the same.

But her heart lifted when she climbed out of the car and Jeremy grinned and winked at her.

Her heart soared again when Daphne failed to lure Jeremy to join her in fishing at the mouth of the river. "I'll stay here with Alice," he said. "She seems to be lucky."

There it was—tantamount to an open declaration of love.

Jeremy and Alice fished amiably, if unsuccessfully, up until lunchtime. Alice had lost her fishing fever. All she wanted was Jeremy's company. But when they broke for lunch, it transpired that Jeremy was still gripped by the desire to catch a fish.

"Where's Daphne?" he said crossly. "I haven't even had a nibble. Maybe I should have gone with her."

"She's at the head of the loch by the river," said Heather.

"If she's still fishing after this time, she must have got something," said Jeremy. "I think I'll go and look."

Heather glanced at Alice's dismal face. "Finish your sandwiches," she said placidly, "and we'll all go and look. Oh, drat, here's the village bobby. Imagine travelling all this way just to scrounge a sandwich . . ."

Hamish sauntered up, red hair and shiny uniform gleaming in the sun.

"How is Major Frame?" asked Alice. "Have they taken him off to Strathbane?"

"No, I thought he would be here by now," said Hamish.

"Here?" shrieked everyone.

"Aye," said Hamish. "They had to let him go. That business where he was said to strangle the club secretary was a bit of a storm in a teacup. The good major was drunk and the secretary objected to the fact that the major hadn't paid his membership fee and seemed to have no intention of doing so. One word led to another and the major attacked the secretary. Several members of the club pulled them apart. The police were called, but no charges pressed. You can't send a man to prison for a murder just because he got drunk and bad-tempered a wee while ago."

"But if he isn't the murderer," said Alice, "who is?"

They all looked at each other in dismay.

Then a faint scream reached their ears, borne on the light breeze.

"Daphne!" said John Cartwright, lurching to his feet. They all scrambled for the loch and waded in. Hamish took off his boots, socks and trousers and, cutting a ridiculous figure in his tunic, cap and underpants, waded into the water after them.

As they ploughed through the shallow loch towards the river, they saw Daphne. Her rod was bent, her line was taut, and she called over her shoulder, "Keep clear! I want to get this one myself."

They all moved forward, however, watching as she battled with the leaping, plunging fish.

"She'll lose it," said Heather. "John, do something."

"Not me," said John. "She wouldn't thank me for any help. Just look at her face!"

Daphne seemed to have aged. Her mouth was clamped tight with deep grooves of strain down either side.

Half an hour passed. Even Hamish, ridiculous in his half dress, stayed where he was. Daphne had played her salmon—for a salmon it was—into the shallow water.

With an exclamation of rage, she suddenly threw her rod down and leapt on the salmon, falling on it in a sort of rugby tackle. Then she rose from the frothing, swirling water, clutching the salmon to her bosom.

She *ran* to the shore, stumbled up the bank, fell and cut her knee, stood up with a great tear across one wader, ran again until she collapsed on the tussocky grass with the writhing fish under her.

They all scrambled to shore. "Let me get the hook out and kill it for you," called John.

"Don't you dare," said Daphne. "That's going to be my pleasure."

They were saved from watching Daphne kill her

fish by a yell from the opposite shore. The major was standing there in full fishing rig.

He waded across to join them.

Hamish watched his approach. He would have expected the major to bluster, to scream about the disgrace of being taken along to the police station, but the major's eyes were riveted on Daphne and her salmon.

"By Jove, where did you get that?"

"Over there," panted Daphne.

"What fly were you using?"

"A Gore Inexpressible. It's one of my father's inventions."

"Where does he fish?"

"He's got an estate in Argyll he uses in the summer. Wouldn't even let me try, which is why I came here. I want one hundred photos to send to him."

Heather opened her mouth to sympathize with the major over his treatment at the hands of the police, but he was already back in the water, a fanatical gleam in his eye, his whole concentration bent on the foaming water.

Then she noticed the still, intent sort of look on Jeremy's face. Oh dear, thought Heather. That remark of Daphne's about her father having an estate in Argyll really got home. Poor Alice.

"Coo-ee!"

The slim figure of Priscilla Halburton-Smythe could be seen on the opposite shore. "Mr. Macbeth," she called.

"Better put your pants on first," said Marvin Roth to Hamish, but Hamish was already off and wading across the loch in Priscilla's direction.

"Sheesh!" said Marvin. "She'll scream the place down when she sees him."

"Your Highlander is very prudish about some things," said Heather. "But any state of undress doesn't seem to embarrass them, and I'm sure the Halburton-Smythes have become used to it by now."

"You're all wet," giggled Priscilla as Hamish waded out. "I came rushing over to tell you that Daddy's in a fearful rage. He's had collect calls from the States and from London. Lucy Hanson, the secretary, accepted the calls and messages thinking they were something to do with the estate. I asked Daddy to give them to me to pass on, but he won't."

"Maybe if we went now we could take a look in the office when he's not around," said Hamish, water dripping down his long, red-haired legs.

"We might be lucky. Everyone's out in the garden having tea. Haven't you got anything to dry yourself with? You look like something out of a *Carry On* film."

"If we open the windows of the car, I'll dry soon

enough," said Hamish. "It is just my legs that are wet. The water did not reach my bum."

"We'll take my car," said Priscilla, "then I'll drop you off back here. Anyone catch anything?"

So as they drove along, Hamish told her about Daphne's catch, and Priscilla threw back her head and laughed. She was wearing a simple pink cotton sheath, and her slim, tanned legs ended in white sandals with thin straps and very high heels. Her legs were like satin. Hamish wondered if she shaved them or whether they were naturally smooth. He wondered what it would be like to run a hand down—or up—all that silky smoothness.

"Stop dreaming," said Priscilla. "We're here."

"I should have put my trousers on at a quiet bit down the road," said Hamish. "But there doesn't seem to be anyone about so I'll just pop them on."

"Well, hurry up. Oh, lor!"

Hamish had got his socks on and had his trousers draped on the gravel drive preparatory to putting them on when Colonel and Mrs. Halburton-Smythe and five guests including John Harrington rounded the corner of the house.

The colonel goggled at Hamish, who stood frozen, one leg in his trousers and one out. He's going to say, "What the hell is the meaning of this?" thought Hamish.

"What the hell is the meaning of this?" screamed the colonel. Mrs. Halburton-Smythe, who was younger than the colonel and had rather pretty, if faded, blonde good looks, shouted, "Come here this minute, Priscilla."

Priscilla thought wildly of the crazy explanations about Daphne's salmon and said hurriedly, "I'll tell you about it later. Get in the car, Mr. Macbeth."

The colonel started his wrathful advance.

Hamish leapt into the car, still half in and half out of his trousers. Priscilla jumped in the other side and they fled off before the colonel could reach them.

"Now I'm for it," said Priscilla gloomily. "He will never listen, you know, which is why no one ever really tells him anything."

Hamish wriggled into his trousers. "And what will you tell your young man? Your father told me—warned me off in fact—that you were about to become engaged."

"I suppose I'd better get engaged to someone," said Priscilla, concentrating on her driving and therefore missing the look of pain on her companion's face. "After all, they did take me to London to do the Season and a fat lot of good that was. It cost them a lot of money. All the other girls seemed content to marry someone suitable.

My friend, Sarah, was wild about this chap, but she married someone else. She said as she walked up to the altar, she thought, 'I wish it could have been so-and-so,' but she's got a baby now and seems pretty happy."

"I should think it would be hell to be married to someone you didn't love," said Hamish, his eyes fixed on the road ahead.

"Really? One never thinks of bobbies as being romantic somehow," said Priscilla carelessly, and the drive back continued in silence.

"Tell your father I caught his poacher," said Hamish, "or rather he left Lochdubh before I could arrest him, but Colonel Halburton-Smythe will not be troubled by that poacher again."

"That might calm him down. I suppose you really have to get those messages. Look, you'd better sneak around about midnight and I'll let you in. I'll try to get them out of the desk for you."

Hamish nodded and raised his hand in a sort of salute as she drove away. He turned his attention to the fishing party. Alice was sitting by the shore of the loch, plaiting a wreath of wild flowers, like some modern-day Ophelia, while Jeremy and Daphne could be seen out in the boat, talking eagerly. There was no sign of the Roths or the Cartwrights. Hamish took off his tunic and, using it as a pillow, stretched his long, lanky length out on the grass. He ran the whole fishing party through his brain, remembering incidents, remembering expressions, remembering what Lady Jane had said. After a time, they all became jumbled together in his head as he fell asleep.

The noise of the fishing party packing up for the day awoke him. The major had caught a salmon, not quite as big as Daphne's, but big enough to make him look as if he had just found the Holy Grail.

Charlie came rushing up. "What did you say to my mother, Mr. Macbeth?"

"There's no use me telling you now, laddie, in case things don't work out. Just say your prayers. Hop in and I'll take you home."

So Alice travelled back with the Cartwrights, worried and lost. If only Jeremy would sleep with her that evening, then she would be sure.

Hamish found Blair waiting for him on his return. The detective was setting out for the hotel for another round of interrogation. Blair was in a fury because he had been so sure at first of the major. He took that fury out on Hamish, calling him lazy, half-witted, and useless, while Hamish stood stolidly to attention, his mind obviously elsewhere.

Blair was also at his worst with the members of the fishing party that evening. They huddled together at dinner, all now wishing they could go home. Blair had said that they might leave on the Sunday morning but that they could expect further calls from the police when they got home.

No one even had the heart to raise a smile at Marvin Roth's appearance. The American had arrived at dinner in full Highland dress, from plaid and kilt to skean-dhu in his stocking top.

Hamish decided to pass the evening hours by going for a long walk. There was no hope of using the phone in his office, since Blair had announced his intention of staying there himself most of the night to sift through the evidence again and make phone calls.

Alice waited in her room after dinner. And waited.

Jeremy was drinking with Daphne in the bar. At last, he escorted Daphne to her room and leaned against the door post and smiled at her. "Are you inviting me in?" he asked.

"No," laughed Daphne. "Not tonight, Napoleon. I've got a headache."

Jeremy stood frowning after she had shut the door. Anxiety gnawed at him despite the amount of gin he had drunk. He went slowly along to a room further along the corridor and rapped on the door.

"Open up, Alice," he said. "It's me."

HAMISH FOUND HIS steps leading back to the scene of the murder. He shone his torch here and there among the bushes, not much hoping to find anything, since the police had already been over the ground very thoroughly.

He suddenly switched off his torch and stood very still. Up above the pool, in the little glade where the fishing party had sat after the discovery of the murder, a twig snapped. He began to move very silently in the direction of the glade, walking in the long grass beside the path so that his feet would make no sound. There was something ancient and eerie about the Highland silence. The night was very still. He stopped at the edge of the glade. A small moon shone down through the trees. Bars of light cut across the scene.

Moving through the flickering bars of light, crouched low like some jungle animal, was Amy Roth. Her restless hands searched the grass.

"Good evening, Mrs. Roth," said Hamish.

Amy stood up slowly and turned to face him, her face a white disc in the shadow.

"Who is it?" she whispered.

"Constable Macbeth."

"Oh." She gave a little laugh and brushed nervously at her clothes. "I lost my lighter. It's gold. I thought I might have left it here."

"A funny time and a scary place to come looking for a lighter," said Hamish. "Why are you *really* here?"

"It's late," she said, moving towards him. "I'm going back to the hotel."

"How long is it since you have suspected your husband of the murder?" asked Hamish.

Amy put her hands to her face. "Marvin can be so violent," she whispered. "But he couldn't... surely..." With a gasp, she thrust past him and fled down the path. Hamish watched her go and shook his head. He had only been guessing, but his remark seemed to have struck gold. He shone his torch around the glade and then decided to examine the ground about the pool before finishing his search. He searched and searched about the ground and the bushes when something caught his eye. He forced his way into the undergrowth and shone his torch. A strand of blue material was caught on a thorn. Strange that the forensic men had missed it.

He carefully took it off the thorn and examined it. It was of a powder blue colour and made of acrylic. He remembered Alice had been wearing a blue trouser suit on the first day of the fishing class.

He sat down thoughtfully by the pool and turned the scrap of material over between finger and thumb. But someone very recently had been wearing just such a colour. His hand suddenly clenched, and he was seized with a feeling of fear and dread.

"Oh no," he whispered.

Day Seven

*The test of an experienced angler is
his ability to play a good sized fish on
average or light equipment.*

—Gilmer G. Robinson, *Fly Casting*

At three minutes after midnight, Hamish parked his car well away from the Halburton-Smythe castle and finished his journey on foot. He was wondering whether to risk trying the door and finding his own way about when it opened and Priscilla whispered, "Hurry up, before we wake the whole house."

She led the way up flights of stairs to her bedroom. She was wearing a white cotton nightgown and negligee, very unrevealing, but Constable Macbeth felt he had never seen such a seductive-looking outfit in his life.

"Now," said Priscilla, sitting down on the bed

and patting the space beside her, "I managed to get into the estates office when they were all jawing about your inquiries at dinner. Mummy believed my story. She said it was just the sort of hare-brained thing you *would* do. There are the messages, but they're in Miss Dimwit's shorthand."

Hamish took the notes. "I do shorthand myself, Miss Halburton-Smythe. But whether I could read this. Yes, I think..."

"Are you asleep, Prissie? I want to talk to you."

"Daddy," squeaked Priscilla. "Into bed, quick, and under the blankets. As far over by the wall as you can get."

Hamish was fortunately not in uniform. The night was warm so he was wearing a checked cotton shirt and an old pair of flannels.

He leapt into bed, under the blankets, and crouched down. Priscilla got in beside him and leaned against the pillows. "Come in!" she called.

Hamish lay very still with his head under the blankets. His face was pressed against Priscilla's thigh. He tried to move it away and she slapped the top of the bed-clothes as a warning to him to lie still.

Colonel Halburton-Smythe came into the room. He sat down on the edge of the bed, and Priscilla shifted to make room for him. She was jammed against Hamish, who felt like groaning.

"Look, pet, the Harringtons might leave tomorrow for the simple reason that you won't come to the point," he heard the colonel say. "Harrington's a fine young chap. It's not as if you're in love with anyone. You can't go on turning down one fellow after another."

"I could get a job, Daddy."

"Nonsense. Marriage and children's the only career for a woman. What will I tell the Harrington's?"

"Tell them anything," yawned Priscilla "I'm so beastly tired, Daddy. I promise I'll be nice to John tomorrow if you'll just go away."

"Very well," said the colonel. "But don't keep him waiting around too long."

At last, to Hamish's intense relief, he heard the door close. Priscilla threw back the bedclothes and looked down at Hamish's ruffled red hair.

"You look quite sweet without that horrible uniform on," said Priscilla. "You must have been nearly suffocated. Your face is all red and you're breathing like a grampus."

"I'm all right," said Hamish, sitting up with an effort. "Let me have a look at those notes."

Priscilla took them out from under her pillow and handed them to him. He frowned as he studied them, and then his face sharpened. "I've got to use the phone," he said.

"You look terrible," said Priscilla. "What is it? Why can't you use the phone at that police station of yours?"

"Blair's there and probably all night. Can I use the one in the estates office?"

"Yes, so long as no one discovers you." Priscilla felt rather sulky and wondered why. "I wouldn't have thought you were so keen on your job."

"Aye," said Hamish, climbing over her to get out of bed. "I'll just creep down the stairs. No one will hear me."

"Good night," said Priscilla crossly.

Hamish smiled down at her as she lay against the pillows. "Thank you for all you have done, Miss Halburton-Smythe." He bent suddenly and kissed her on the cheek, turned red as fire, and fled from the room.

"Well, well," thought Priscilla. She put a hand up to her cheek and stared in a bemused way at the closed door.

Hamish sat beside the phone in the estates office and in his head turned over the names of his many relatives. There was Rory in London, Erchie in New York, Peter in Hong Kong, Jenny in Aylesbury, which was near enough to Oxford...

At last, he picked up the phone and began to dial.

                    *   *   *

A PALE DAWN was lighting up the sky and the water as Hamish Macbeth wearily made his way along the waterfront. There was something he had to do before he went to sleep and it was something that only duty was prompting him to do. His heart felt heavy, and his lips moved in a soundless Gaelic prayer.

He turned in at a white-painted gate and went around the back of the house to the kitchen door. He rapped loud and long on the glass until he saw a light go on upstairs. He waited, hearing footsteps descending, shuffling footsteps approaching the kitchen door.

The door opened and Tina Baxter stood blinking at him nervously. She clutched a pink woollen dressing gown tightly at her neck. All colour drained from her face.

"Aye, it's me," said Hamish heavily. "Mind if I come in?"

She stood aside, and he walked past her into the kitchen. She followed him and sat down at the kitchen table as if her legs could no longer bear her weight.

"I was here earlier," said Hamish, "talking to you about young Charlie's future. You were wearing a blue dress." He took an envelope out of his tunic pocket and extracted the piece of material he had found on the bush beside the pool. "Is this yours?"

"Yes," whispered Mrs. Baxter. She covered her face with her hands and began to cry.

"I couldn't help it," she sobbed. "The disgrace. My Charlie's name in the papers. I had to shut her mouth."

Hamish sat down opposite her. His head was beginning to clear, and his earlier fright was beginning to recede as common sense took over. The first rays of sun began to warm the kitchen.

"Mrs. Baxter," he said gently. "Immediately after the murder all the bushes and braes and heather and trees were combed for clues by the forensic boys. It's awfy strange they didn't find this and I did."

"I did it." Tina Baxter stared at him, her face working.

"Aye, that you did. Not the murder. You cut a bit out of your dress and left it there, hoping someone would find it. So now we'll have another wee chat about Charlie. He's twelve years old. *Twelve years old.* Just think o' that. He's a strong boy but there is no way he could have overpowered a woman of Lady Jane's size. Then there's the lad's character..."

"It's bad blood, bad blood," said Tina Baxter, her hands clutching and unclutching the material of her dressing gown. "His father was violent. He threatened to kill me if I didn't give him a divorce." Her voice was rising hysterically.

"I am thinking," said Hamish sincerely, "that you would drive a saint to violence. I feel like striking you myself. Do you know that because of your silly clue-planting you had me thinking you knew that Charlie did it and were trying to fix the blame on yourself? You're a dangerous woman. Now, here's what you are going to do. You are going to leave Charlie here to stay with his aunt and I suggest you go back home and see one o' thae head doctors. You'll drive the bairn mad with all your hysterics.

"If you don't do what I say, I will let the newspapers know that you believed your own boy capable of murder and nearly got him accused of it by your clumsiness."

Hamish rose to his feet. "So think on that, Mrs. Baxter. I'll bring mair scandal down on your head than you ever could hae imagined."

IT WAS THE last day of the fishing course. Unless the police requested otherwise, Blair would take their home and business addresses and allow them to leave on the Sunday morning. The river Anstey was still closed to them. Heather and John had suggested they fish the Marag.

On returning to the police station, Hamish found

that Blair was still asleep. He typed up his notes, studied the results, and then put them to one side. He thought long and carefully about each member of the fishing school. He decided he was being haunted by the scale of the crime. He began to read through his well-thumbed ten-volume edition of *Famous Crimes*. Motives tumbled one after another before his tired eyes. Murder for money, for passion, for revenge. Alcohol or drugs brought out the Hyde side of the character, but no one in the fishing school case drank daily to excess and not one of them had shown any sign of being a drug user. He made one pot after another of strong tea. His dog, Towser, prowled about uneasily, stopping to lick his master's hand as if wondering what was keeping him from his bed, for Towser liked to stretch out on the bed at Hamish's feet.

"It is all a matter of lack of conscience," thought Hamish.

By the time the little fishing class was setting out for their last day, Hamish was sound asleep, his dog snoring at his feet, and a sheaf of notes clutched to his chest.

He was awakened by Blair shaking his shoulder. "It's noon," snarled Blair savagely. "By God, I'll report you for sheer laziness. I've got a job for you. You'll come along with me to that hotel this evening and you'll take down the addresses of the whole lot of 'em. I don't just mean their home addresses, we've got those. I mean where they work and where they're likely to be visiting."

"Get out!" said a small, shrill voice behind Blair. The large detective swung around in amazement. Charlie Baxter stood in the doorway clutching a mug of tea. "This is Constable Macbeth's house," he said, "and you've got no right to bully him."

Blair stared at the boy, who was white with anger.

Hamish, who had fallen asleep in the shirt and flannels he had worn the night before, swung his legs quickly out of bed.

"Into the kitchen with you, Charlie," he said. "What time will you be wanting me at the hotel, sir?"

"Six o'clock," snapped Blair. "And tell that kid to mind his manners." He stomped off where he could shortly be heard haranguing MacNab and Anderson in Hamish's office.

"I've prepared breakfast for you, Mr. Macbeth," said Charlie shyly. "It's on the table."

"Aye, you've done very well," said Hamish, tucking into charred bacon and rubbery egg. "Quite the wee housewife. Aren't you going fishing?"

"I thought you might run up to the Marag with me," said Charlie. "You see, I have to thank you.

Mother left in a rage. I don't know what you said or what Auntie said to her afterwards, but I'm to stay."

"Isn't that the great thing," smiled Hamish. "Och, your ma's a decent body, but she worries overmuch about everything."

"Perhaps we'll catch the murderer together, Mr. Macbeth."

"We might at that. Wait till I put on my uniform and we'll be off."

There was a festival air about the fishing school. Even Daphne seemed to have stopped her bitchy behaviour. All of them had come to the conclusion at breakfast that none of them had done it and Lady Jane had probably come across a poacher or some itinerant madman. Tomorrow, they would all return home with a story they could dine out on for years.

Alice drew Hamish aside and showed him a silver and cairngorm ring she was wearing on a string around her neck. "Jeremy gave this to me," she said. "He bought it at the gift shop this morning. I was going to put it on my finger, but he said to keep it secret for the moment."

"Why?" asked Hamish curiously. "It is not as if the man is married."

"Oh, you men are so secretive," laughed Alice.

"If I were to be married to the lady of my

choice," said Hamish slowly, "I would shout it from the mountain top."

But Alice only giggled happily and walked away. Hamish went to sit on a rock where he could get a view of everyone in the fishing school and there he stayed for the whole of the day. At last, at five o'clock, he walked up to Heather and said, "You are all expected in the hotel at six o'clock, Mrs. Cartwright. They will want to wash and change. Mr. Blair wants me to take your names and addresses, and myself will be having a bit of a word with you."

"All right," said Heather, looking curiously at Hamish's face. "I'll get them together."

"I will go on," said Hamish, "and make sure that no other guests are allowed in the lounge."

At the hotel, Hamish found Blair, MacNab and Anderson waiting for him. "They are coming," said Hamish, "and will be in the lounge at six. I am just going to tell Mr. Johnson to keep other guests out of the lounge. You see, I am going to find your murderer for you, Mr. Blair."

MacNab sniggered, and Jimmy Anderson said, "You've been reading too many detective stories, Hamish. Great detective gathers suspects in the library and unmasks killer."

"Aye, chust so," said Hamish, walking off.

"He's mad," growled MacNab. "I'll tell him to go home and have some black coffee."

"No," said Blair. "Let him get on with it. I want him to make a right fool of himself. I'll have him out of his cushy job in a week."

And so Hamish found Blair surprisingly mild and cooperative when he returned. Yes. Blair grinned. MacNab would guard the door and Anderson the window.

At last, one by one, the members of the fishing party entered the lounge. Hamish stood with his back to the empty fireplace and waited until they were all seated.

"Before I take down your addresses and send you on your way tomorrow," he said, "there's just a few things I have to say." MacNab stifled a laugh.

"It was a wee bit difficult for me to see at first which one of you had done the murder because you all seemed to have a motive."

"Get on with it." Daphne Gore yawned. "I'm dying for a drink."

"John and Heather Cartwright," went on Hamish, ignoring the interruption. "A bad press might have ruined your school, and there was no doubt that Lady Jane meant to give you a bad write-up. You had a letter from friends in Austria telling you how she had managed to ruin *them*. Mr. Cartwright lives for this fishing school and Mrs. Cartwright lives for her husband. Both could have committed the murder...or one of them.

"Marvin and Amy Roth..."

"I'm not going to listen to any more of this," said Heather. She half rose from her chair, her face flushed with distress, changed her mind, and sat down again, looking not at Hamish, but at her husband.

"Marvin Roth," said Hamish, "was involved in a scandal some years ago when he was charged with running sweatshops in the garment district of New York and employing illegal aliens. He did not want his past raked up just when he was set on entering politics, and he guessed from a remark Lady Jane made that she knew all about his past.

"Then Amy Roth. Always talking about being a Blanchard from Augusta, except you aren't a Blanchard by birth. You married Tom Blanchard ten years ago and the marriage only lasted a few weeks, but you kept his name and background. Lady Jane must have known that."

Marvin polished the top of his bald head. "Look here," he said desperately. "Amy didn't say anything about being a Blanchard by birth, now did you, hon?"

"Oh, yes, she did," said Daphne. "Right down to the last mint julep."

"You misheard," said Marvin, giving Daphne a cold, pale look.

"Then we come to Major Peter Frame," said Hamish.

"Not again," said the major, burying his face in his hands.

"You care very much for your reputation as an officer and a gentleman," said Hamish. "You have an excitable temper and you were heard to threaten Lady Jane's life. You were never in the war, nor have you a particularly upper-class background. Lady Jane gave you a rough time.

"Alice Wilson." Alice smiled tremulously at Jeremy, who frowned and looked at the door. "You got into minor trouble as a child and it's plagued you ever since. There was a big reason why you did not want the matter to get out. Perhaps you might have killed because of it."

Nobody moved, but they seemed to shrink away from Alice.

"I wouldn't," gasped Alice. "Jeremy, please . . ."

"Charlie Baxter," went on Hamish. "Well, you had a bad time with her ladyship, and boys of your age can do terrible things under stress.

"Jeremy Blythe. I think you are a ruthless, ambitious, selfish man. You messed up two women in your Oxford days and God knows how many more.

You want to be elected a member of the Conservative party, and Lady Jane's story, had it appeared, would have meant the end of your ambitions."

"This is cruel," thought Alice wildly. "He could have taken us aside one at a time. It's like some horrible game of truths, bringing all our skeletons out of the closet." She looked angrily at Hamish, who was consulting a sheaf of notes. He raised his eyes and looked around the room. "He doesn't know who did it!" thought Alice with a sudden flash of intuition. "He's looking for some sign that will betray the murderer."

"Daphne Gore. Lady Jane knew all about you. I won't go into the details of your background that landed you under psychiatric care, but I think you are unbalanced enough to kill someone, given enough stress."

There was a shocked silence. "If your little game is over, Macbeth," said Blair, "we'll get those addresses and..."

Hamish ignored him.

"Now we had one clue, a torn corner of a photograph with part of the legend BUY BRIT—in one corner. At first I thought it might be part of an old Buy British poster. The fragment also shows the top of a head with something sparkly on it like a tiara. I made a lot of phone calls and found out at last what the legend really read.

"It runs BUY BRITTELS BEER—a kind of beer that is sold in America."

"Never heard of it," said Marvin Roth.

"Not many people have," said Hamish. "It was made locally by a small firm controlled by the Mafia in the Red Hook section of Brooklyn. It was so strong the locals said it was made out of all the bodies that didn't end up in the East River. It was a bit of luck I found that out. Mrs. Roth had muttered something about Red Hook, but at the time, I thought she must be talking about something to do with the fishing. It was only later I remembered Red Hook was a district in Brooklyn. I have a cousin, Erchie, who lives in Red Hook and I phoned him up. He said it was sold in small Mafia gambling clubs.

"He neffer heard of Amy Blanchard or Amy Roth, but he had heard of an Amy a whiles back who was a stripper, Amy not being a usual name in the Italian section. Now Lady Jane had been in the States, no doubt digging up what dirt she could. Lady Jane was content to wait until her column appeared to see the rest of you suffering or to imagine your suffering. But Amy caught her on the raw. She arranged to meet Mrs. Roth in the woods. There she showed her a photograph of Amy the stripper, wearing very little except a spangled headdress. You, Mrs. Roth, have very little in the way of a conscience. This is something I *feel* about you, rather than something I definitely know. It came on me bit by bit. The look in the back of your eyes always had a certain steady calculating hardness no matter what you were saying. So you strangled her and then you dragged the body to the pool. You wanted something to weight the body and so you went down to the beach and found some old rusty chain. As soon as you had pushed her into the pool, you felt safe. You then returned to her room and destroyed all her notes and papers. Your husband would never know you were a Brooklyn stripper who sold her favours."

Good God, thought Heather Cartwright wildly. Do people still talk about women selling their favours?

Amy Roth sat very still, her eyes lowered.

Marvin lumbered up and sat on the arm of his wife's chair and put a hand on her shoulder and gave it a comforting squeeze.

"You're talking shit," grated Marvin. "I won't believe what you said about Amy. I'll tell you something else. She knows I love her. She knows that I wouldn't give a damn about her past. Mine ain't so lily white. Where's your proof?"

"She was seen," said Hamish. "There is this poacher, Angus MacGregor..."

His voice trailed away as Amy raised her eyes and looked at him. Her eyes had lost their soft, cow-like expression. They were as flat and as hard as two stones.

"You did it, didn't you?" said Hamish.

Amy Roth moistened her lips.

"Yes," she said flatly.

"And when you said you thought your husband had done it and you were frightened he had left something incriminating behind, you were really frightened *you* had left something."

"Yes," said Amy again in that dreadful flat voice.

Marvin's face was white and working with emotion. Tears started to his eyes. "You're making her say all this." There was a long silence. "Amy," pleaded Marvin, "if you did it, you did it for me. Well, the hell with politics. I wasn't ever sold on the idea anyway."

"That was not the reason, was it, Amy?" said Hamish.

"I guess not," she said in a dull voice. She stretched her fingers and looked at them thoughtfully. "She messed with me, that's all. I don't like no one messing with me."

And as Anderson and MacNab closed in on her, she gave her husband an apologetic little smile.

*   *   *

HAMISH LEANED ON the harbour wall, keeping his eyes fixed on the sea. He felt immeasurably tired. He did not want to see Amy dragged out to the police car. She would be taken to the women's prison at Strathbane.

He waited a long time while cars came and went. Then he heard Blair's voice behind him. "That was a neat bit of work, Constable. I suppose you're laughing your head off. MacNab and Anderson have taken her to Strathbane with the rest of my men. I'm just about to follow. Fine reading it will make for my superiors. Case solved by the village bobby."

"Och, no," said Hamish soothingly. "It was yourself that pointed the way. I will not be taking any credit."

"Why did you keep this poacher witness up your sleeve? It worked the trick."

"I chust made that up," said Hamish, lighting a cigarette. "It was all guesswork."

"What!"

"Aye. I just took a chance. You see, Erchie told me that the only Amy he had ever heard of around the Mafia clubs away back was a young stripper. He was not sure it was the same person, at all, at all. I just thought I would chance it."

"But what if you had been wrong?"

"Aye, well, I have no doubt you would have had me out of my job as you were hoping to do. Now Amy had been a bit of a prostitute as well. I noticed that she was always restless. That's the thing about prostitutes. They can cover up the past with a layer of ladylike veneer, but they never lose that hunted, fidgety air."

"You having great experience of the breed," said Blair sarcastically.

Hamish blushed. "No, no. But there was Jessie over in Aberdeen who married that man on the council...Then there was how Amy behaved at dinner. I couldnae help noticing that she would pour round the wine without waiting for the waiter or the men to do it."

"Must have been a shock for old Marvin."

"Aye, it was that. I first started to think it might be her when I looked at her wrists. They're very strong for a woman. But it was her eyelids that clinched the matter."

"Her *eyelids*?"

"They are strained a bit at the corners. I have always noticed that criminal-type women have this feature."

"Mr. Roth has gone with her. He's going to get some big-shot lawyer."

"Aye, love is a terrible thing," said Hamish mournfully.

"I think you were damn lucky," said Blair sourly. "I can't believe you're not going to take any credit for this."

Hamish turned and leaned his back against the harbour wall. "Oh, you can believe it. I have no mind to leave Lochdubh. But if you were to put a little something in your report about my hard-working, if unintelligent, help, that would be just fine."

Blair smiled slowly and clapped Hamish on the shoulder.

"I think we've time for a drink, Hamish," he said. "Let's go into the bar."

Epilogue

Sunday morning. All the survivors chattering and laughing over the breakfast table. Oh, the relief to have it all cleared up and be able to go home. Reporters and photographers waited outside the courtyard of the hotel. But it would be possible to drive straight past them. Only John Cartwright knew that the major had already been out to talk to them. The major was back on form, so much so that he could not bear to admit that the case had been solved by the village constable but merely paused in his bragging to say that he was jolly glad the police had cleared the matter up.

John sighed. The other guests, the new fishing school, would be arriving later in the day. Not one had cancelled. They would survive.

Alice smiled radiantly at Jeremy. He had not visited her last night, excusing himself by saying he was all washed up with all the drama of the arrest.

She was wearing the ring he had given her on her engagement finger.

"Hope to see you all again," said Major Peter Frame cheerfully. "Better be on my way."

"I'd better get my traps too," said Jeremy.

"My suitcase is at the reception so I'll have another cup of coffee and wait for you here," said Alice sunnily. Jeremy put a hand briefly on her shoulder.

"Better get mine as well," said Daphne languidly, "and get my fish out of the freezer. Hope it'll fit in the car."

The Cartwrights said goodbye and went off to look at equipment for the new members of the fishing school.

Alice sat alone. It was a beautiful day and she sipped her coffee and looked happily out at the sun sparkling on the loch. Perhaps she and Jeremy would return on their honeymoon.

All of a sudden she stiffened. Daphne had said something about hoping her fish would fit in the car. Which car? There was really only room for two in Jeremy's sports car.

She rushed out to reception and grabbed her suitcase and ran out into the courtyard. Jeremy and Daphne were laughing as they tried to find room for Daphne's enormous salmon.

"Jeremy," cried Alice. "I thought we were going back together."

He strolled over to her. "No, it's only fair I should give Daphne a lift back. After all, we did travel up together."

"But we're engaged," shrieked Alice. "Look! I'm wearing your ring."

"It was only a present," mumbled Jeremy. "I mean, I didn't ask you to marry me, did I?"

"You *slept* with me," said Alice, beginning to sob. "I might be pregnant." She threw her arms around Jeremy's neck.

"Good God," he said. He jerked her arms down and ran for his car. Daphne was already sitting in the passenger seat.

Jeremy climbed in and slammed the door just as Alice ran up. Her hands scrabbled at the window as he let in the clutch. The smart red sports car gave a growl and swept off.

Alice became aware of the press watching curiously from outside the courtyard and some of the hotel servants watching as well.

She picked up her case and, with her head held high, she walked back into the hotel.

HAMISH AND CHARLIE rowed slowly back to Lochdubh after an afternoon's fishing. They had caught four mackerel and two ling. Charlie had lost his hard, calculating stare and was looking out at the world with dreamy pleasure.

"There's Mr. Johnson waiting for you," he said as they approached the shore.

Hamish was sharply reminded of the time when they had last returned and Blair was waiting for them.

"Where have you been?" asked Mr. Johnson as soon as Hamish landed on the beach. "I've been going out of my wits. That girl Alice Wilson had a scene with Mr. Blythe and she's disappeared. Her case is still at the reception and she hasn't booked in for another night. The staff have been out searching for her."

"You run along home," said Hamish to the boy. "Don't worry, Mr. Johnson. I'll find her."

"Where would she go?" thought Hamish as he drove up the twisting road out of Lochdubh. "I suppose she might just keep on walking and walking."

He drove on through the pale Highland twilight, his eyes searching from left to right of the road.

He was ten miles out of Lochdubh when his sharp eyes suddenly spied what looked like a black lump on a black rock. He drove on and parked the car around a bend in the road. Then he began to walk back to the rock, his shoes making no noise on the springy heather.

Alice sat on the rock, a picture of abject misery. She was not crying, having cried all day until she could cry no more, but she was hiccupping with dry sobs.

Hamish sat down beside her. "Only a fool would cry for someone who didn't really want them."

"Go away," said Alice, turning red-rimmed eyes to his.

"No, I will not go away. You are coming with me. You have caused enough worry and trouble this day. And all over some pipsqueak you didn't even love."

"I love him," wailed Alice.

"No, you don't. Went to bed with him, didn't you? Aye, I thought as much. So now you've got to pretend you love him. Och, lassie, it's your pride that's hurt, not your heart. There's one silly woman charged with murder and all because of damned snobbery and here you are planning to jump in the nearest loch as soon as you get up the courage so as to make a rat like Blythe sorry."

"I . . . I didn't . . . I wouldn't."

"Look, I tried to tell you he was a snob. As soon as he decided Daphne was rich enough, he decided to settle for her. She'll marry him. That kind always get what they want and they'll have a dead-alive sort of marriage. You only wanted the dream, Alice. Be honest and admit it's over."

"What if I'm pregnant?"

"Face that when it comes. When's your next period?" asked Hamish.

"Next week, I think."

"Well, you'll maybe just be all right. Come along with me and I'll get us a drink. You're a pretty girl and you're young."

"Do...do you think I'm pretty?"

"Very," lied Hamish gallantly. "Smashing little thing, that's what I thought when I first saw you."

He helped her to her feet and put an arm about her shoulders and together they walked towards the road.

"It's a grand evening to be alive," said Hamish. "Just think about that."

Down below them, the lights of the village twinkled in the half dark. The twilight was scented with thyme and pine and heather. A rocketing pheasant whirred up from a clump of heather at the other side of the road. Out in the loch, the fishing boats were chugging out to sea.

Hamish pulled Alice to the side of the road as he heard a car approaching. A Rolls, black and sleek, slowed. Inside sat Priscilla Halburton-Smythe. She was wearing a white evening dress and a diamond necklace sparkled against her breast. Beside her at the wheel was John Harrington. Priscilla looked at

Hamish, at Hamish's arm about Alice's shoulders, shrugged, and said something to John, who looked across her at Hamish and Alice and laughed. Then the car sped away.

Alice took a deep breath of clean-scented air. She was feeling better already. Hamish's arm was comforting. She glanced up at him. He really wasn't bad-looking. His eyelashes were very long for a man and his hair was a fascinating colour of red. "You're right," said Alice. "Only a fool would cry for someone who didn't really want them."

Hamish watched the tail lights of the disappearing Rolls-Royce. "Did I say that?" he asked, and then added in so low a voice that Alice could not hear what he was saying, "If I said that then I am a very great fool indeed."

He helped Alice into his car but he sat for a few moments, staring straight ahead.

"I've always wondered, Mr. Macbeth," said Alice timidly. "What's a FEB?"

Hamish let in the clutch. "Fucking English Bastard," he said. And with an angry screech of tyres he swung the car around and they plunged down into the heathery darkness of the road leading to Lochdubh.

SAVOR THE FLAVORS OF SCOTLAND—
WITH ANOTHER
HAMISH MACBETH MYSTERY
BY **M. C. BEATON!**

*Please turn the page
for a preview of*

Death of a Policeman

A watched pot never boils.

—Mid-nineteenth-century proverb

The fact that all the police forces in Scotland were to be amalgamated into one large force struck terror into police headquarters in Strathbane. It was said that all over Scotland three thousand auxiliary jobs would be lost, which would mean more work for the actual police themselves. Then they would start chopping heads of the very police force itself.

Only one man was happy about the news— Detective Chief Inspector Blair. Surely this might be the opportunity to get rid of Police Sergeant Hamish Macbeth and winkle him out of his cosy station in Lochdubh. He could not understand how Hamish had been able to hang on with local police stations closing down all over Scotland.

But he experienced a setback when he broached

the idea to his chief, Superintendent Daviot. "Sutherland is a huge county," said Daviot, "and it is surely economical to have Macbeth cover all of it."

"But most of the time, he and his sidekick, Fraser, just mooch around doing nothing," complained Blair.

"We have no proof of that," said Daviot severely. "You should be worried about your own job."

"Whit!"

"I am sure we will have officials soon crawling all over us to see what they can cut," said Daviot.

Blair took himself off to the pub to crouch over a double whisky and try to work out a plan. If he could prove that Hamish Macbeth did little, then he could send a report in to the new authorities. But who would be low enough to spy on Macbeth?

After another double whisky, his brain seemed to clear. Cyril Sessions was a fairly new constable, nicknamed Romeo because of his good looks. Shortly after his arrival from Perth, Blair had uncovered evidence that Cyril had been enjoying the favours of a prostitute, without paying her a penny. She had finally cracked and reported Cyril. Blair got the complaint and confronted Cyril. Cyril had pleaded and begged and said he would do anything if Blair made the complaint go away.

Cunningly, Blair decided to keep this ally in the

bank, so to speak, until such time as he would need to draw on him. He phoned headquarters and asked Cyril to join him.

Women in the pub stared appreciatively at Cyril when he entered. He was of medium height with glossy black hair, blue eyes in a square handsome face, and a muscular figure.

"Sit down, my lad," said Blair. "I've a wee job for you. I want evidence that Hamish Macbeth in Lochdubh does bugger all when it comes to policing."

"Isn't that the man who's got a grand reputation for solving murders?"

"It was me that solved them," said Blair, "while that slimy toad took the credit. You owe me a favour, or do I need to remind you that I had to threaten that brass nail to keep her painted mouth shut?"

"Brass nail?"

"Where have you been? Brass nail. Screw. Get it? That prossy you were banging."

"Oh, aye. That."

"Aye, that. Here's what you've got tae do. Take a fishing holiday in Lochdubh and get photos of Macbeth lounging around. His policeman, Dick Fraser, often sleeps in a deck chair in the front garden. Get a good shot o' that. Macbeth doesn't know you, so you can get real close. Chat with the locals. Pick up gossip."

"I don't fish."

"Well, rambling or something like that. The highlands are fu' o' hairy-legged bastards farting ower the hills."

"When do I start?"

"Next week'll do. I want this done and dusted before numpties from the new police arrangement descend on us."

Cyril looked at him shrewdly. "Have you tried this before?"

Blair shifted his fat haunches on the barstool. He had, in fact, and it had ended with his spy nearly getting killed. But he had no intention of telling Cyril anything about it.

"No, just thought o' it," he said. "Get moving and fix that holiday."

HAMISH WAS ACTUALLY working at that moment. Lairg sheep sales are the biggest in Europe and he was policing them with Dick at his side. Because of the size of the sales, Strathbane had sent up two policemen to assist him. The importance of the yearly event meant that crofters were often dressed in the sort of finery people thought were the reserve of tourists: deer stalkers, tall crooks, kilts and sporrans.

Hamish and Dick strolled into the beer tent late

in the day and found their other two colleagues. "Everyone upset about the new Scottish police force?" asked Hamish, joining them.

"You can say that again," said one of them. "Take off the civilian staff, and think o' the extra paperwork."

"And how's my dear friend Blair?" asked Hamish.

The other policeman sniggered, "I think he's in lurv."

"Who's the lucky lady?"

"It's a bloke. Fairly new copper called Cyril Sessions. Real handsome chap. Blair's been seen drinking with him all over the place. Can't get enough of his company."

As THEY WALKED out of the beer tent, Dick said sententiously, "It does happen, you know."

"What does?" asked Hamish.

"Fellows when they get on a bit. They wake up to the fact that they prefer other blokes to their missus."

"Oh, aye? Well, the only love affair Blair's ever had is with the booze. He's plotting something."

"Do you mind if I hurry off?" said Dick anxiously. "I'm due down in Strathbane."

"Another quiz?"

"Aye, and the prize is a brand new Volvo."

"Off you go. Things are quiet here."

HAMISH SWITCHED ON the television that evening. Dick had such a reputation for winning quiz competitions that he was surprised they let him on.

The questions seemed to be very difficult. Six contestants were quickly whittled down to two, Dick and a shabby old man. And then Dick lost at the last question: how long does it take light from the moon to reach the earth?

The old man said quickly, "One-point-twenty-six seconds." There was a roll of drums and cheers from the audience as he was led to the gleaming new car.

Hamish waited up until a weary Dick arrived home. "Not like you to lose," said Hamish. "That must be the first time."

"I couldnae do it to him," said Dick.

"What?"

"He was an auld crofter. He'd never been on one of thae quiz shows before. The stories o' hardship he told me in the green room. It would ha' been wicked not to let the poor auld soul win."

"What was his name again?"

"Henry McQueen. Got a bittie o' a place outside Bonar Bridge."

"I wonder if there's anything on the computer about him," said Hamish.

"Why?"

"Just a hunch. I've got a feeling I saw him at the sheep sales."

Dick followed Hamish into the police office. Hamish switched on the computer and searched for Henry McQueen's name. "There's something here from last year's *Highland Times*," said Hamish, clicking it open. "There you are. I thought I'd heard of him. He took top price for his lambs two years running. You were conned. Oh, here's another link. Five years ago he came out top on *Mastermind*. Subject, the Epistles of St. Paul."

"I'll murder the auld creep," raged Dick.

"Oh, leave it. I'm sure he'll crop up again," said Hamish soothingly, "and then you can wipe the floor with him."

THE FOLLOWING DAY, Cyril checked into Mrs. Mackenzie's bed and breakfast on the waterfront at Lochdubh. He dumped his haversack in a small room and wondered how long he could put up with pretending to be a rambler, particularly as he had arrived in his car. He had pointed out to Blair that he was surely not going to be able to follow Macbeth around on foot.

The room was at the back of the house. It was cold. There was a meter on the wall with a sign saying that pound coins had to be deposited for electricity. The bed was narrow and covered in rough blankets under a pink candlewick spread. A print of Jesus feeding the multitude with loaves and fishes hung over the blocked-up fireplace. Underneath was the legend "His Eye Is on the Sparrow." On a rickety table by the bed was a large Bible. The room was fairly dark. Cyril popped a coin in the meter and switched on the light in a glass bowl above his head full of dead flies. He hung his clothes in the curtained alcove that served as a wardrobe. There was neither a phone nor a television set. The only reason, he thought, that she got any customers was because Mrs. Mackenzie charged cheap rates.

He decided to go out for a walk around the village and start work.

The day outside was warmer than his room. A pale October sun shone down on a row of whitewashed cottages fronting the sea loch. It looked like a picture postcard. Cyril walked towards the harbour. He brightened when he saw a pub. He would start with a drink and see what he could find out from the locals. There was a silence when he entered. He ordered a vodka and tonic.

A small man in tight clothes materialised at his elbow and said, "Are you on holiday?"

"Yes," said Cyril. "I'm Jamie Mackay up from Perth."

"Archie Maclean," said the little man.

"Let me buy you a drink," said Cyril, "and maybe we could sit over at that table by the window. I'd like to get to know a bit about the village."

Archie ordered a double whisky. Cyril realised that Blair had said nothing about paying for his work. Conversation rose again as they made their way to the table.

"So what are you doing here?" asked Archie.

"I came up by car, but I might do a bit of walking."

Archie's sharp blue eyes in his nut-brown face dropped to look at Cyril's highly polished black shoes. "I hope you've got boots with you," he said. "You won't get far in those."

"Yes, I've got boots," said Cyril. He wondered why the little man wore such tight clothes, not knowing that Archie's wife washed all his clothes so that they shrank.

"So, much crime around here?" asked Cyril.

"No, it's fair quiet."

"I saw a police station. Not much for a copper to do up here."

"Hamish Macbeth, the police sergeant, covers a

big part o' Sutherland," said Archie. "He's got a lot tae do. Thanks for the drink, laddie. Got tae go."

HAMISH WAS SEATED at the kitchen table when Archie burst through the door. "What's up?" asked Hamish.

"'Member the time when that scunner Blair put a copper on yer tail to report on ye?"

"As if it were yesterday," said Hamish. "Has he sent another?"

"Could be," said Archie, sitting down at the table. "Could I hae wan o' your espresso coffees? The wifie doesnae hold wi' coffee."

"That's Dick's machine. I don't know how to operate it. I'll fetch him. He's sleeping in the garden."

Hamish strolled round to the front of the police station just in time to see the tall figure of Cyril snapping a photograph of Dick asleep in his deck chair. He nipped round onto the road and confronted Cyril. "What's so special about a photograph of a man in a deck chair?" asked Hamish.

"I'm a bit of an amateur photographer," said Cyril. "I thought I'd enter it for a competition and call it 'Sleeping Policeman.'"

"Visiting?"

"Yes. Good place for walks."

"Where are you staying?" asked Hamish.

"Mrs. Mackenzie's. I'll be getting along."

Cyril strode off. Hamish stared after him. Then he went into the office and phoned detective Jimmy Anderson.

"How are things up in peasantville?" asked Jimmy.

"Weird."

"It's aye weird up there."

"There's this fellow turned up and took a photo of Dick asleep in the garden. Handsome chap with curly black hair, tall, blue eyes, little half-moon scar above the right eye, but with policeman's shoes on and black socks. Says he's going to be going for walks. Anyone missing from headquarters that looks like that?"

"There's one smarmy bastard who sucks up to Blair. Cyril Sessions."

"I knew it!" exclaimed Hamish. "Blair is out to get proof that there's no crime up here. I'll get that photo back somehow."

Hamish woke Dick up and explained the situation. He ended by saying, "Let's see if we can lose the cheil for an hour. Give Archie a mug o' espresso first."

They walked over to the harbour fifteen minutes later, where Archie Maclean was sitting on a bollard, rolling a cigarette. "No tourists today?" asked Hamish. Fishing stocks were dwindling, and so

Archie supplemented his income by taking tourists on trips round the loch.

"I've only got a couple. They'll be along in a minute."

"Do me a favour. Yon chap you met in the pub is one o' Blair's snoops. He'll be hanging around. He's staying at Mrs. Mackenzie's. Offer him a free trip in your boat."

"Aye, right. Want me to tip him ower the side?"

"No, just keep him away. If he's got his camera with him, try to stage an accident to the camera that makes it look as if it's his fault."

ARCHIE SCURRIED OFF. He found Cyril outside Mrs. Mackenzie's. Cyril was delighted to accept. It would be a chance to find out more about Macbeth.

Hamish stood at his living-room window, watching, until he saw the fishing boat sail out into the loch. Then he hurried along to Mrs. Mackenzie's bed and breakfast.

Before he got there, he met the Currie sisters, twins Nessie and Jessie, on the waterfront. They were very much alike. Although the day was sunny, there was a nip in the air, and so they had reverted to their winter wear of camel-hair coats, headscarves, and brogues.

"Grand day," said Hamish. "Have you seen the newcomer?"

"We have that," said Nessie. "Like a fillum star."

"Fillum star," echoed the Greek chorus that was Jessie.

"It's refreshing to find a young man who kens so much about the Bible," said Hamish. "He's out with Archie, but when he gets back, you should invite him to tea. Right religious, he is."

"We'll do that," said Nessie. "It will be nice to talk to a clean young man instead o' a lazy philanderer like yourself."

"Like yourself," came her sister's echo.

Hamish walked on and knocked at the door of the bed and breakfast. Mrs. Mackenzie was a small woman wearing a flower-patterned overall with her hair tied up in a headscarf. The lines on her face were permanently set in disapproval.

"Whit?" she demanded.

"I would like a look at the newcomer's room," said Hamish. "We've had a tip-off."

"Then he can pack his bags and get out."

"No, no," said Hamish soothingly. "Don't tell him I called. Chust a routine enquiry. You don't want to go losing a paying customer at this time of year. Chust a wee peek in his room."

"Oh, all right. Top o' the stairs on the left. The door isnae locked. I was up there cleaning."

Hamish nipped up the stairs and into Cyril's

room. There was a computer lying on the bed, but what he wanted was the camera. There was no sign of it. He could only hope that Archie would find a way to get rid of it.

ARCHIE LET HIS mate, Ally Harris, take the wheel while he pointed out various landmarks to the two tourists, a husband and wife, and Cyril. Cyril was standing at the side of the boat, his camera slung round his neck.

Moving behind him, Archie took out a sharp knife and sliced almost through the strap at the back of Cyril's neck.

He said, "If youse will look ower the side, that's where the kelpie is supposed tae live."

"What's a kelpie?" asked the female.

"It's a creature that appears as a sea horse and sometimes changes into a beautiful wumman," said Archie. "It goes after wee bairns. It gets them to stroke it and it's adhesive and when they stick to it, it drags them down into the loch and eats them. It's supposed to live right down there. Lean right ower and you'll maybe see it."

Cyril and the tourists leaned over. "There is something down there," said Cyril excitedly. A black shape could be seen moving in the murky depths. His camera was swinging from his neck by the strap. Just as he was reaching for it, the strap broke and his camera dropped down into the water.

A seal surfaced and stared up at them as Cyril let out a wail of dismay.

"You should ha' got yourself wan o' thae wee yins you can carry in your pocket," said Archie. "I hivnae seen wan like that in years. If you go to Patel's shop, you can buy wan o' thae cheap throw-away ones."

"It was a friend's camera," said Cyril. He cursed Blair, who had given him an old Rolleiflex camera out of storage at headquarters, saying it was better than any newfangled one. He did have a Canon pocket one inside his jacket. At least he would be more comfortable using that.

ARCHIE TELEPHONED HAMISH to say that Cyril's camera was now somewhere at the bottom of the loch, and Hamish heaved a sigh of relief.

Before, when he had been under threat, he had manufactured a crime wave with the help of the locals. But Hamish was feeling lazy, enjoying the rare good weather of the autumn.

CYRIL HAD READ up on Hamish's successful cases and knew that several had taken place in the town of Braikie. The following day, he decided to visit the town, hoping the residents there might have less favourable ideas about Hamish than the villagers had. He had gone to the village stores and after leaning on the counter, talking about the weather, he had asked the owner, Mr. Patel, what he thought of the local policeman. Mr. Patel had smiled and launched on a paean of praise about Hamish.

Cyril had then gone to the Italian restaurant for dinner and quizzed the waiter, Willie Lamont. His heart sank when it turned out that Hamish was godfather to Willie's child. Was no one going to criticise the man?

But in Braikie, his hopes sank lower. The people he talked to did not know Hamish personally but knew his reputation for solving murders and seemed to be proud to have such a policeman looking after them.

He was passing the library when he noticed a sign outside saying there were books for sale. Cyril decided to buy some light reading and walked into the Victorian gloom of the building.

Hetty Dunstable, the librarian, saw a handsome man looking around and teetered forward on her high heels. "Can I help you?"

Cyril saw a small, thin woman in her early forties wearing a nearly transparent white blouse over a tight skirt. She had a small, pinched face and bulging brown eyes. Cyril thought sourly that she looked like a rabbit with myxomatosis. But he gave his most charming smile and said, "I saw that you had books for sale."

"Yes, they're over here," said Hetty, leading the way to a wooden bench. "These are the ones that are too damaged to remain on the shelves. Are you new to the area?"

"Just on holiday," said Cyril. "I'm over in Lochdubh."

"Keep clear of the police station. Hamish Macbeth is useless."

"I'd like to hear more," said Cyril. "I enjoy a bit of gossip with a pretty girl. When do you get off?"

"We close up in ten minutes."

"Let's go for a drink."

"Yes, I would love that," said Hetty.

HETTY HAD NO intention of telling this gorgeous man her real reason for disliking Hamish. She had once invited Hamish to a party at her flat after having met him on one of his investigations. Hamish was not interested. But she had drunk too much and had thrown herself at him, calling him her darling. Hamish had gently pushed her away and gone home. Her friends teased her about it until she began to think Hamish had wronged her. She told them so many times that Hamish had led her on that she began to believe it.

CYRIL WAS OFTEN seen in Hetty's company in the following days. Then, to Hetty's dismay, he said he would be too busy to see her. Hetty began to feel guilty. She was sure Cyril was spying on Hamish and wondered if he was a villain. She had made up a lot of malicious stories about Hamish's laziness. If anything happened to Hamish, the investigation would lead back to her.

She at last phoned Hamish and said someone called Jamie Mackay had been asking a lot of questions about him.

"Don't worry," said Hamish. "I know all about him," correctly guessing that Jamie was Cyril.

"What will you do?" asked Hetty.

"Take my shotgun and blow the bugger's head off," said Hamish and rang off.

"LET'S GIVE CYRIL something to do tomorrow," Hamish said to Dick. "We'll race off tomorrow up north and give the lad something to chase. The beasties are getting fat. They need some exercise."

Hamish's "beasties" consisted of a wild cat called Sonsie and a dog called Towser. "I'll get a picnic ready," said Dick.

Hamish felt a stab of irritation. He wished Dick would not be so—well—*domesticated*. He felt Dick was taking the place of a possible wife, and Hamish often dreamed of marriage. His love affair with television presenter Elspeth Grant had recently fallen through. He had once been engaged to Priscilla Halburton-Smythe, daughter of the retired colonel who owned the Tommel Castle Hotel. But Priscilla's sexual coldness had caused him to break off the engagement.

AT THAT MOMENT, Cyril was ensconced in the Currie sisters' parlour, balancing a cup of tea on one knee. He had hoped the sisters would give him some gossip about Hamish, but they seemed hell-bent on quizzing him about the King James Version of the Bible.

"Beautiful words," said Nessie. " 'I am the voice of one crying in the wilderness.' "

"I couldn't agree more," said Cyril, ignoring Jessie's echo. He thought, If I don't get out of this damn place soon I'll go mad. "You were saying something about the local policeman."

"No, I wasn't," said Nessie.

"Bit of a layabout, is he?"

"We do not gossip in this village," said Nessie righteously. "Pass me the Bible, Jessie, and we'll hear this nice young man read to us."

It was a large Victorian Bible, illustrated with steel engravings. Feeling trapped, Cyril began to read, and, as he read, he began to experience a strange feeling of doom. His mobile phone suddenly rang, and he grabbed it out of his pocket. It was Blair, asking if there was any progress.

"Can't talk now, Mother," said Cyril. "I'll call you later." He rang off.

"You shouldn't cut your mother off like that," chided Nessie.

"How right you are." Cyril stood up and put the Bible and his cup on the table. "I'll get back to my digs and call her from there."

"We'll see you in the kirk on Sunday," said Nessie.

If I'm still alive and not dead with boredom, thought Cyril, making his escape.

"WHERE ARE WE off to?" asked Dick the next morning as he climbed into the Land Rover beside Hamish.

"Do you know Sandybeach?"

"No, where's that?"

"Tiny little place up north of Scourie. Grand place for a picnic. I'll put the siren on and get Cyril chasing us."

"It's only seven in the morning," said Dick. "Think he'll be up yet?"

"Probably not. But I've phoned Jimmy. Blair's bound to ask if there's been a report of a crime, so I told him to say there was a burglary at Sandybeach."

"So what do we do if the scunner catches up with us?"

"He won't. It's so quiet up there, you can hear a car coming for miles. We'll take off for somewhere else."

THE SOUND OF the siren woke Cyril. He tumbled out of bed and dashed to the window, opened it, and hung out. He could just see the Land Rover racing out over the humpbacked bridge. He scrabbled into his clothes and phoned Blair, asking him to find out where Hamish had gone.

He had gone a mile out of Lochdubh when Blair rang. "Burglary at a place called Sandybeach."

"Where's that?"

"How should I know? Look at a map."

Cyril programmed his sat-nav and set off in pursuit. He hurtled along the one-track roads, blind to the beauty all around him. Purple heather blazed on the flanks of the soaring mountains. Rowan trees shone with bloodred berries. Above, the sky was an arch of blue. At one point, he thought he heard the sound of another driver behind him and suddenly stopped, switched off his engine, rolled down the windows, and listened. But there was nothing to be heard but the mournful call of a curlew.

Cyril crouched over the wheel and drove on.

Sutherland, the southland of the Vikings, is the most underpopulated county in the British Isles. The west coast has the most dazzling scenery. But to Cyril, it was an odd foreign landscape, alien, far from the bustle and crowds of Strathbane.

At long last, he saw a signpost pointing the way to Sandybeach.

"The end of the road," said Cyril, not knowing that, for him, it was.

SAVOR THE FLAVORS OF SCOTLAND—
WITH ANOTHER
HAMISH MACBETH MYSTERY
BY **M. C. BEATON!**

*Please turn the page
for a preview of*

Death of Yesterday

Send home my long stray'd eyes to me,
Which O! too long have dwelt on thee

—William Blake

Morag Merrilea was an art student, earning money in her summer holidays by working as a secretary for Shopmark Fashions in Cnothan in the Scottish county of Sutherland. She was English and considered herself a cut above her fellow workers. She was highly unpopular. Her appearance was unprepossessing. She had lank brown hair and rather prominent green eyes. But she had a passion for art and for studying faces.

Shopmark Fashions was a new factory on the outskirts of the village, risen out of an old derelict Victorian furniture store. Cnothan was a grim place, with one main street running down to a man-made loch over which towered the grey walls of a hydro-electric dam.

Morag had taken the job because she had dreamt of a romantic highland village, and had never quite got over the culture shock of being in Cnothan where the sour locals took pride in "keeping themselves to themselves."

SHE SAT IN her usual corner of the Highlander pub one Saturday evening with her sketchbook, busily drawing the faces of people in the pub, and, also, the face of someone looking in at the window. Morag always drank alone. The other employees of the factory drank at a pub down on the lochside and, strangely enough, Morag's solitary drinking was not remarked on because of her unpopularity and the locals shying away from any mention of her.

Although not particularly imaginative, she seemed that particular evening to feel the remoteness, the very foreignness of Sutherland pressing in on her, a claustrophobic sense that the great towering mountains were creeping closer across the heathery moors. The result was, she drank more than usual. The pub was quite full with forestry workers, crofters, and the unemployed. Morag was brilliant at drawing faces and felt the very act of drawing people and putting them on paper put them in her power.

At one point, she went to the lavatory. When she returned, she found her sketchbook was missing. She complained to the barman and to everyone around. Getting nothing in reply but blank stares, she downed her drink and made for the door. Morag collapsed outside and was taken to hospital.

After she came awake the following morning and received a lecture from a young doctor on the evils of drink, Morag was gripped with a sudden fear that she might be an alcoholic. She had drunk four pints of beer and assumed she had experienced a blackout. She could not remember yesterday evening at all.

She did have one friend at Hornsey Art College, where she had studied. She phoned her friend, Celia Hedron, and told her about losing her memory.

Celia said sharply, "Have you considered that someone might have slipped you a date rape drug? That blacks you out so you can't remember things."

This dramatic solution appealed to Morag, who did not like to think she was a common alcoholic. She dithered for a week before catching a bus from Cnothan and presenting herself at the police station in Lochdubh. She had been told that the police sergeant, Hamish Macbeth, was also responsible for policing Cnothan—along with vast tracts of Sutherland.

HER FIRST IMPRESSION of Hamish Macbeth was a bad one. When she arrived, he was up on a ladder clearing out the guttering. His lazy constable, Dick Fraser, a plump man with a grey moustache, was sleeping peacefully in the front garden on a deck chair.

"You!" shouted Morag. "Get down here immediately. I have a crime to report."

Hamish came slowly down the ladder. She saw a tall man with flaming red hair and hazel eyes.

"What seems to be the problem?" he asked.

Morag threw back her head and declared, "I have been drugged, raped, and my sketchbook has been stolen."

"Then you'd better come ben to the office," said Hamish mildly.

"Whassat?" mumbled Dick and went back to sleep.

Hamish led the way in at the side door, through the kitchen and into his small office, where he pulled out a chair for her. He wrote down the details of her addresses in Cnothan and London along with her phone numbers at home and work.

"It's like this," said Morag. She gave him her view of what had happened, along with details of her age, twenty-three, and her work as a secretary at the clothes factory.

"And when exactly did this take place?" asked Hamish.

"Last Saturday week."

Hamish had been taking notes. He put down his pen. "If you were drugged with some date rape drug, it would no longer be in your system. Were you checked for signs of rape?"

"Well, no."

"I think we should go to the hospital right away and have you checked."

Morag bit her lip. She had examined herself and knew there were no signs of bruising or forced entry. "I can't be bothered," she said.

"Then I don't see what you expect me to do," said Hamish patiently.

"You are a moron," said Morag. "You could at least make some push to get my sketchbook back—that is if you ever get off your arse and do anything."

"What were you sketching?"

"Faces of people in the pub. Oh, and someone who looked in at the window."

"Are you any good?" asked Hamish bluntly.

She opened her large handbag and pulled out a small sketchpad and handed it to him.

His interest quickened. She was very good indeed.

"I'll need to take a note of who was in the pub. Can you remember any names?"

"They're all just faces to me—Angus this and Jimmy that. I do not consort with the local peasantry. The factory staff drink at the Loaning down on the loch."

"With an attitude like that," said Hamish, the sudden sibilance of his accent showing he was annoyed, "I'm fair astounded that someone didnae try to bump you off instead of chust slipping something in your drink."

"You're as useless as the rest of . . ."

"Calm down, lassie. I hae this idea . . ."

"Wonders will never cease."

"Oh, shut up and listen for once in your life. I know a hypnotist down in Strathbane. He might be able to put you under and restore some o' your memory."

Morag's protruding eyes gleamed. The drama of such a suggestion appealed to her, along with the idea of rattling the cage of whoever had drugged her drink.

"I'll make an appointment and let you know," said Hamish.

*   *   *

HAMISH WONDERED AS he set off for Strathbane later that day with Dick why he was even bothering to help such an unlovely character as Morag Merrilea. He cursed himself for not having asked exactly how much she had to drink. She could simply have had an alcoholic blackout.

Still, he reminded himself, he wasn't doing anything else at the moment. The summer was unusually warm with those nasty biting midges of the Highlands out in force. Patel's, the local shop in Lochdubh, had sold out of insect repellent.

As they mounted a crest of the road, Dick said, "Every time I see Strathbane, I'm right glad I'm out of it."

Strathbane was a blot on the beauty of Sutherland. Once a busy fishing port, it had died when the fishing stocks ran out. Drugs arrived, and it became a town with an air of dirt and desolation.

"I don't like this idea of a hypnotist," said Dick. "Sounds awfy like black magic."

"Och, even Strathbane police use Mr. Jeffreys from time to time."

"Did they say they would pay his bill?"

Hamish shifted uncomfortably in the driver's seat. He knew that Detective Chief Inspector Blair, the bane of his life, would have put a stop to it.

"It's fine," he said airily. "He'll just send in his bill as usual."

DICK WAS DISAPPOINTED in Mr. Jeffreys. He had expected to meet an elderly guru.

But Jeffreys was only in his thirties, a thin man with brown hair in a ponytail, dressed in torn jeans and a T-shirt.

"Let me see," said Jeffreys. "I can fit her in at three o'clock next Saturday."

Hamish phoned Morag on her mobile. She was delighted. "Wait till those bastards in the pub hear about this!"

"I wouldnae go around shooting your mouth off," cautioned Hamish. "I'll collect you on Saturday and take you to Strathbane."

IN THE THREE days leading up to Saturday, Hamish and Dick pottered around the police station. To Dick Fraser, a portly man with a grey moustache, it was paradise. Viewed as useless by headquarters in Strathbane, he had been relocated to Lochdubh. He was a quiz addict, appearing on television quiz shows, and the kitchen in the police station gleamed with his winnings—an espresso coffee making machine, a dishwasher, a new washing machine, and a new microwave.

The single and widowed ladies of the village began to regard him as prime husband material, but Dick showed no interest, preferring to dream in a deck chair in the front garden by day and watch television in the evenings.

He was roused from his lethargy on Saturday by Hamish. "We'd better go and pick up yon Morag female," said Hamish. "Get your uniform on."

Morag rented a flat in a Victorian villa on the edge of Cnothan. When Hamish rang her doorbell, there was no reply. Morag's flat was on the top floor. He stood back and looked up. The curtains were open but there was no sign of anyone moving about.

"Silly cow," he muttered. "I'm sure she wouldnae have forgotten." He rang the landlady's bell.

Mrs. Douglas, the landlady, opened the door. She was a small round woman with thick glasses and an untidy thatch of grey hair.

"Whit now?" she demanded.

"We've come to collect Miss Merrilea," said Hamish patiently. "Is herself at home?"

"Dinnae ken."

"Would you please go and look?"

Grumbling, she shuffled off up the stairs. They waited in the warm sunlight.

At last she reappeared and handed Hamish a postcard. "This was stuck on her door," she said.

Typed neatly on a postcard was: "Gone to London. Will be in touch." It was not signed.

"I don't like this," said Hamish. "Would you mind showing us her flat?"

"Have ye a warrant?"

"No, I haff not!" said Hamish. "But if you don't let me in and show me her flat, I'll come back here with a warrant and I will turn this whole damn place upside down, including your premises."

"Here, now, no need for that," she said, thinking of the cash undeclared to the taxman hidden under her mattress. "I'll get the key."

They followed her into a shadowy hall lit with coloured harlequin diamonds of light from the sun shining through the stained-glass panel on the front door.

Dick eyed the steep stairs. "I'll be waiting for ye outside, sir," he said to Hamish.

"Oh, all right," said Hamish crossly.

He followed Mrs. Douglas as she panted up the stairs. She inserted a key into a door on the top landing. "There's no need for you to wait," said Hamish. "I'll bring you down the key when I've finished."

The flat consisted of a small living room, a cell of a bedroom, a kitchen unit behind a curtain, and a shower. The living room contained a small card table laden with artist's materials and two hardback chairs by the window. There was a dingy print of *The Stag at Bay* over the empty fireplace. One battered armchair was beside the fireplace facing a small television set. Planks on bricks along one wall supplied bookshelves.

Hamish went in to the bedroom. He opened the wardrobe. A few skirts and blouses hung there and a winter coat. On top of the wardrobe was a large suitcase. He hauled it down and opened it up. It was empty. He put it back and then opened a chest of drawers. There were various surprisingly saucy items of lingerie: thongs and stockings with lace tops.

He sat down on the bed and looked round. She might have had a backpack of some kind to take a few clothes with her. There was no sign of a handbag, passport, or wallet.

He locked up and went downstairs to where Mrs. Douglas was waiting in the hall. "Did she have a car?" he asked, handing over the keys.

"No, she had a bike."

"And where does she keep it?"

"Just outside. But it's no' there."

"When did you last see her?"

"Cannae bring tae mind."

"Think!"

"Oh, I mind now. It was yesterday morning. Herself was just off tae work."

"Was she carrying a suitcase or any sort of luggage?"

"No. She just got on her bike and went off, same as ever."

Hamish felt uneasy. He put the postcard in a forensic bag and went out to join Dick.

"We'd better check where she works," he said. "I've got a bad feeling about this."

AT SHOPMARK FASHIONS, they found that Morag worked as secretary to the boss, Harry Gilchrist. Mr. Gilchrist kept them waiting ten minutes, which Hamish put down to the usual pompous Scottish boss's way of trying to seem important.

Mr. Gilchrist was a tall thin man in his forties. He had thick black hair in a widow's peak above a sallow face and wet brown eyes.

"Working on Saturday?" asked Hamish.

"Work never stops," said Gilchrist. "What do the police want with me?"

"Did Morag Merrilea turn up for work yesterday?"

"As a matter of fact, she didn't. I meant to send someone to check on her on Monday if she was still absent."

"She left a postcard on the door of her flat saying she had gone to London."

"Isn't that just typical of staff these days!" raged Gilchrist. "Well, if you come across her, tell her she's fired."

"Did she say anything about going to see a hypnotist?"

"No. A hypnotist? Why?"

Hamish explained about the suspected drugged drink and the missing sketchbook.

"Oh, that? She was complaining about that all over the place. She did drink a fair bit. She was in the habit of making things up."

"Is there anyone she was close to?"

"She kept herself to herself."

Like the whole of bloody Cnothan, thought Hamish.

DICK AND HAMISH next went to the Highlander pub. Pubs all over Britain had been smartened up with restaurants and pleasant décor, but the Highlander had been unmoved by time. There was one dim room with scarred tables and rickety chairs. The walls were still brown with nicotine from the days before the smoking ban. The only food on offer was in a glass case on the counter: tired-looking sandwiches and a solitary mutton pie.

Hamish recognised the barman and owner, Stolly Maguire. Stolly was polishing a glass with a dirty rag when they approached him. He was a thickset man with a bald head with a tank top strained over a beer belly.

Hamish explained they were trying to find out the whereabouts of Morag Merrilea.

"Thon artist?" said Solly. "Havenae seen her. Usually comes in Saturday evening."

"Two Saturdays ago," said Hamish patiently, "did you notice anyone approaching her table when she went to the toilet?"

"Naw. It was fair busy."

Hamish turned round and surveyed the customers, a mixture of crofters, shepherds, builders, and the unemployed.

"Which one of them was here two Saturdays ago?"

"I cannae mind," said Stolly. "Ask them? I saw her collapsing outside the door and phoned for an ambulance."

So Hamish and Dick went from table to table to receive surly answers to the effect that they had seen her on that Saturday but hadn't noticed anyone taking her sketchbook or putting something in her drink.

But a youth with greasy hair said he had noticed

a stranger. "Can you describe him?" asked Hamish. "What is your name?"

"Fergus McQueen."

"Well, Fergus, what did he look like?"

"Hard tae tell. He had wan o' thae baseball caps pulled right down. Small and skinny."

"What was he wearing?"

"Black T-shirt, black jeans."

"The cap. Did it have a logo on it?"

"Naw. It was dark green with an orange stripe."

"Give me your address. We may want you to come to Strathbane and help a police artist make a sketch."

BACK AT LOCHDUBH, Hamish sat down at the computer in the police station office and sent over a report. He felt uneasy. It was too much of a coincidence that she should disappear when she had an appointment with the hypnotist.

To his amazement, he got a call from Detective Sergeant Jimmy Anderson later that day. "Blair's decided to look into it," he said.

"Why? I thought he'd delight in shooting the whole thing down," said Hamish.

"I think he feels if there is a crime, then he wants to be the one to solve it. You've stolen his glory too many times."

"I'd better get back to Cnothan and join him."

"He says you're to sit tight and look after your sheep and leave it to the experts."

Hamish groaned. He knew that Blair's blustering, bullying tactics would make the locals clam up even more.

HAMISH WAITED GLOOMILY for the inevitable. Sure enough, it came later with an e-mail from Blair telling him it was a wild-goose chase and to stop wasting police time and, furthermore, never again try to employ the hypnotist without first getting clearance.

Undeterred, Hamish went back to Cnothan, knocking on doors, questioning one after the other without success.

He was furious when he returned to Lochdubh to receive a phone call from Superintendent Daviot. The locals in Cnothan had complained of police harassment. Blair had found nothing. Hamish was to leave it all alone.

THE WEATHER WAS unusually hot. Three weeks after the disappearance of Morag Merrilea, two men were loading bales of T-shirts onto a lorry outside Shopmark Fashions when they suddenly stopped their work.

"Thon's an awfy smell from that bale," said one, "and it's heavy, too."

"Better cut it open," said his companion. "There's maybe a dead animal inside."

They sliced the twine that held the bale and unrolled it.

The dead and decomposing body of Morag Merrilea rolled out and lay under the eye of the glaring sun.

O the disgrace of it!—The scandal,
the incredible come-down!

—Sir Max Beerbohm

Hamish Macbeth awoke to another day. His dog, Towser, was lying across his feet, snoring rhythmically. Sunlight slanted through the gap in the curtains. The telephone in the police office part of the house shrilled and then the answering machine clicked on. He should rise and go and find out what it was. It was his duty as a police constable of the village of Lochdubh and part of the surrounding area of the county of Sutherland. But all he wanted to do was pull the duvet over his head and go back to sleep.

He could not really think of any good reason for getting up to face the day.

He had, until his demotion from sergeant back to

constable and the end of his engagement with Priscilla Halburton-Smythe, daughter of a local hotelier, been very popular, a happy state of affairs he had taken for granted. But somehow the story had got about that he had cruelly jilted Priscilla, she who had been too good for him in the first place, and so, when he went about his duties, he was met with reproachful looks. Although Chief Superintendent Peter Daviot had also been angry with him over the end of the engagement, that was not why Hamish had been demoted. He had solved a murder mystery by producing what he firmly believed was the body of the murdered man to elicit a shock confession from the guilty party. The ruse had worked, but he had had the wrong body. It had turned out to be a fine example of Pictish man and the police were accused of being clod-hopping morons for having so roughly handled and used such a prime exhibit. Someone had to be punished, and naturally that someone was Hamish Macbeth.

Hamish was not an ambitious man. In fact, he was quite happy with his lot as ordinary police constable, but he felt the displeasure of the village people keenly. His days before his disgrace had pleasantly been given up to mooching around the village and gossiping. Now no one seemed to want to spend the time of the day with him, or that was the way it seemed to his gloomy mind. If Priscilla, whom Hamish considered remarkably unaffected by the end to the romance, had stayed around to demonstrate that fact, then he would not be in bad odour. But she had left to stay with friends in Gloucestershire for an extended visit, so as far as the villagers were concerned, Hamish had driven her off and she was down in "foreign" parts, nursing a broken heart.

Mrs. Halburton-Smythe did not help matters by shaking her head and murmuring "Poor Priscilla" whenever Hamish's name was mentioned, although what Mrs. Halburton-Smythe was sad about was that she was beginning to believe that her cool and aloof daughter did not want to marry anyone.

With a groan, Hamish made the effort and got up. Towser gave a grumbling sound in the back of his throat and slid to the floor and padded off towards the kitchen.

Hamish jerked back the curtains. The police station was on the waterfront and overlooked the sea loch, which lay that morning as calm as a sheet of glass.

He washed and dressed and went through to the police office. The message was from headquarters in Strathbane reminding him he had not sent in a full statement about a break-in at a small hotel on the road to Drum. He ambled into the kitchen and made himself a breakfast of bread and cheese, for he had forgotten to light the stove. Priscilla had presented him with a brand-new electric cooker, but he had childishly sent it back.

He fed Towser and stood on one leg, irresolute, looking like a heron brooding over a pond. Depression was new to him. He had to take action, to do something to lift it. He could start by typing that report. On the other hand, Towser needed a walk.

The phone began to ring again and so he quickly left the police station with Towser at his heels and set out along the waterfront in the hot morning sun. And it was hot, a most unusual state of affairs for the north of Scotland. He pushed his peaked cap back on his fiery-red hair and his hazel eyes saw irritation heading his way in the form of the Currie sisters, Jessie and Nessie.

The eyes of the village spinsters constantly accused him of being a heartless flirt. He touched his cap and said, "Fine morning."

"It is for some. It is for some," said Jessie, who had an irritating habit of repeating things. "Some, on the other hand, are breaking their hearts."

Hamish skirted round them and went on his way. Resentment and self-pity warred in his bosom. He had once helped the Currie sisters out of a dangerous jam and had destroyed evidence to do so. Damn it, he had helped a lot of people in this village. Why should he be made to feel guilty?

His thoughts turned to Angela Brodie, the doctor's wife. Now *she* had not turned against him. He walked up the short path leading to the doctor's house, went round the back and knocked at the kitchen door. Angela answered it, the dogs yapping at her feet. She pushed her fine wispy hair out of her eyes and said vaguely, "Hamish! How nice. Come in and have coffee."

She cleared a space for him at the kitchen table by lifting piles of books off it and placing them on the floor.

"I don't seem to have had a chat with you in ages," said Angela cheerfully. "Heard from Priscilla?"

Hamish, who had just been lowering his bottom onto a kitchen chair, stood up again. "If you are going to start as well..." he began huffily.

"Sit down," said Angela, startled. "Start what?"

Hamish slowly sat down again. "You haff been the only one who hass not gone on about Priscilla," he said, his Highland accent becoming more sibilant, as it always did when he was angry or upset.

"Oh, I see," said Angela, pouring him a mug of coffee and sliding it across the table towards him. "I only asked about Priscilla because I assumed that you and she were still friends."

"And so we are!" said Hamish. "But ye would-nae think so with this lot in Lochdubh. You would think I wass some sort of Victorian philanderer the way they go on."

"It'll blow over," said Angela comfortably. "These sort of ideas spread through these villages like an infection. Mrs. Wellington started it." Mrs. Wellington was the minister's wife. "She started it by complaining that you were a feckless womanizer and things like that. You know how she goes on. But you brought that on yourself!"

"How?"

"She happened to overhear you doing a very good impression of her to delight the Boy Scouts."

"Ah."

"And so she got a resentment to you and shared it around. Resentment is very infectious. It has always fascinated me the way, for example, one malcontent can bring a whole factory out on strike and keep everyone out on strike until the firm folds and they all lose their jobs. Also, you're going around being so gloomy. That fuels it. You look like a guilty man."

"I'm a bit down," confessed Hamish. "The fact is I've taken a scunner tae Lockdubh and everyone in it."

"Hamish! You love the place!"

"Not at the moment."

"You're due some leave, aren't you? Get right away on holiday. You could get one of those cheap holidays in Spain. Or some of the African package holidays are very cheap."

"I'll think about it," said Hamish moodily. "I might just take a wee holiday somewhere in Scotland, seeing that the weather's fine."

Angela got up and began to rummage through a pile of old magazines on a kitchen chair. She extracted a battered Sunday-paper colour supplement. "What about this place?" she said, flipping open the pages. "Skag. Have you been to Skag?"

"That's over on the Moray Firth. I havenae been there, though I've been into Forres, which is quite close." He looked at the coloured photographs. It looked like a Cornish resort with long white beaches, pretty village and harbour. There was also a page of advertisements for hotels and boarding-houses in Skag. "I'll take this with me, Angela, if you don't mind."

"Keep it," said the doctor's wife. "It's one less piece of junk. I can never bring myself to throw magazines out or even take them along to the waiting-room."

"What's the latest gossip?" asked Hamish.

She sipped her coffee and looked at him in that

vague way she always had. Then she put down her coffee-cup and said, "Well, the biggest piece of gossip apart from yourself is Jessie Currie."

"What about her?"

"Angus Macdonald, the seer, told her she would be married before the year's out."

Hamish's hazel eyes lit up with amusement. "She didnae believe him, did she?"

"She says she didn't, but she's been casting a speculative eye over the men of the village and Nessie is worrying about being left alone."

"And who is this charmer who's going to sweep our Jessie off her feet?"

"Angus will only say it's going to be a divorced fisherman."

"We don't have any divorced fishermen!"

"I pointed that out to Jessie and she said, 'Not yet.'"

"Chance'll be a fine thing," said Hamish. "Dried-up old spinster like her."

"Hamish! That's cruel."

"Aye, well, she should mind her own business instead of ither folks'."

"I really do think you need to get away. Willie Lamont was saying the other day that when you go to the restaurant, you're always complaining about something."

Willie Lamont, Hamish's one-time sidekick, had left the police force to marry a young relative of the owner of the Italian restaurant and worked there much harder than he had ever done when he was a police constable.

"The portions are getting smaller and smaller and the prices higher."

"Still, it's not like you to complain. I'll bet if you had a break from all of us, you'd be very happy to come back and see us again."

Hamish got up. "We'll see. Thanks for the coffee."

He walked along the waterfront and perched on the harbour wall. Towser sighed and lay down. Hamish studied the magazine article. There was an advertisement from a boarding-house called The Friendly House "situated right on the beach with commanding sea views, old-fashioned cooking; special low terms for July, halfboard."

Hamish lowered the magazine and looked over at the village. It was a largely Georgian village, built all in the same year by one of the dukes of Sutherland to enlarge the fishing industry, trim little square whitewashed houses facing the sea loch. He knew everyone in the village, from people who had lived there all their lives like the Currie sisters, to the latest incomers. He felt better now he had talked to Angela, much better. He had been seeing things through a distorting glass, imagining everyone was against him.

So when he saw Mrs. Maclean, Archie, the fisherman's wife, stumping along towards him, carrying a heavy shopping basket, he gave her a cheery smile. "Lazing about as usual?" demanded Mrs. Maclean. She was a ferocious housekeeper, never seen without a pinafore and smelling strongly of soap and disinfectant. Her hair was twisted up in foam rollers and covered with a headscarf.

"I am enjoying the day," said Hamish mildly.

"How ye can enjoy anything wi' that poor lassie down in England eating her heart out is beyond me," said Mrs. Maclean.

Hamish studied her thoughtfully and then a gleam of malice came into his eyes. "Priscilla isn't nursing a broken heart, but some poor fisherman's wife is soon going tae be."

"Whit dae ye mean?"

Hamish slid down from the wall, rolled up the colour supplement and put it in his trousers pocket. "Aye, Angus Macdonald told Jessie Currie she'd be married afore the year was out and tae a fisherman, a *divorced* fisherman. How's Archie these days?"

"Archie's jist fine," said Mrs. Maclean, her eyes roving this way and that, as if expecting to see her husband. It was well known in the village that Archie, when not fishing, spent most of the day avoiding his wife, in case she scrubbed him to death, as he put it. "Anyway, it's all havers," she said. "Jessie Currie. The very idea."

And then, to Hamish's delight, he saw Archie in the distance. He came abreast of the Curries' cottage and Jessie called something to him over the garden hedge and he stopped to talk to her.

"There's your man ower there," said Hamish happily, "and talking tae Jessie."

Mrs. Maclean stared in the direction he pointed and gave something that sounded like a yelp and set off at speed. But Archie saw her coming and left Jessie and darted up one of the lanes leading up to the back village and was gone from view.

Hamish strolled back to the police station, phoned Strathbane and said he wanted to take three weeks' immediate holiday. Permission was easily granted. The bane of his life, Detective Chief Inspector Blair, was in Glasgow, there had been virtually no crime at all for months, and so it was agreed that Sergeant Macgregor over at Cnothan could take over Hamish's duties as well as his own. He was free to leave at the end of the week. He phoned the boarding-house in Skag and learned to his delight that, thanks to a cancellation, they had one room free for the very time he wanted, and yes, dogs were allowed.

Feeling happier than he had felt for some time, he then set out to arrange for his sheep to be looked after, his hens and ducks as well, and then decided to pay a visit to the seer to find out what had possessed the old sinner to wind Jessie up like that.

Angus Macdonald, the seer, a big, craggy man like one of the minor prophets, peered all around Hamish looking for a present before he let him in. The villagers usually brought him something, a bottle of whisky or a cake.

"No, I didnae bring you anything," said Hamish, following him into his small living-room. "I don't want your services. I simply want to know what you were doing telling Jessie she was going tae marry a divorced fisherman."

"I seed it," said Angus huffily. "I dinnae make things up."

"Come on, man. Jessie!"

"Well, that's whit I seed."

"That sort o' rubbish could start gossip."

"Maybe that's whit you're hoping fur, Hamish."

"How's that?"

"Stop them gossiping about you and your lassie."

"I think you're an old fraud," said Hamish. "I've always thought you were an old faker."

"You're jist bad-tempered because ye think nobody loves ye. Here's Mrs. Wellington coming."

Hamish jumped up in alarm. He scampered off and ran down the hill, seemingly deaf to the booming hail of the minister's wife.

"That man," said the tweedy Mrs. Wellington as she plumped herself down in an armchair. "I'll be glad to see the back of him."

"Is he going somewhere?" asked Angus.

"I met Mrs. Brodie just before I came up here. She said that Hamish was thinking of going over to Skag for a holiday."

"Oh, aye," said Angus. "Now whit can I dae for you, Mrs. Wellington?"

"This business about Jessie Currie. It can't be true." Her eyes sharpened. "Unless you've heard something."

"I see things," said Angus.

"And you hear more gossip than anyone I know," said Mrs. Wellington sharply. "I brought you one of my fruitcakes. It's over on the counter. You see, Mr. Patel at the stores told me that he had seen Archie Maclean talking to Jessie Currie and when he saw his wife at the other end of the waterfront coming towards him, he ran away."

"I'm saying nothing," said Angus mysteriously. "But we'll jist have a wee cup o' tea and try that cake."

*   *   *

EARLY ON SATURDAY morning, Hamish Macbeth hung a sign on the door of the police station, referring all inquiries to Sergeant Macgregor at Cnothan. He locked the police Land Rover up in the garage, put Towser on the leash, and picked up his suitcase. Then the phone in the police station began to ring. He decided to answer it in the hope that someone in the village might have phoned up to wish him a happy holiday.

The voice of the seer sounded down the line. "I wouldnae go tae Skag if I were you, Hamish."

Hamish felt a superstitious feeling of dread.

"Why not?" he asked.

"I see death. I see death and trouble fur you, Hamish Macbeth."

"I havenae time to listen to your rubbish," said Hamish sharply and put the receiver down.

At the other end of the line, Angus listened to that click and smiled. Called him a fraud, had he? Well, that should give Hamish Macbeth something to think about!

Hamish left the police station and walked along to the end of the harbour to get the bus to Bonar Bridge. From Bonar Bridge he would get another bus to Inverness and then buses from Inverness over to Skag.

The bus was, as usual, late, twenty minutes late,

in fact. Hamish was the only passenger. He often thought the driver, Peter Dunwiddy, deliberately started off late so as to have an excuse to break the speed limit, even with a policeman on board. Hamish hung on tightly and Towser flattened himself on the floor of the bus as it hurtled up out of Lochdubh and then began to scream around the hairpin bends on its way to Bonar Bridge. He expected to feel a lightness of heart as Lochdubh and all its residents fell away behind him. But he felt an odd tugging sadness at his heart. To match his mood, the day was grey, all colour bleached out of the landscape, like a Japanese print. He hoped the good weather would return. Perhaps he should not have been so parochial as to holiday in Scotland. When did Scotland ever guarantee sunny weather and water warm enough to go for a swim?

By the time he reached the village of Skag, he felt as tired as if he had walked there. He asked directions to The Friendly House and then set out. It was about two miles outside the village, and not on the beach exactly but behind a row of sand dunes set a quarter of a mile back from the North Sea.

It was an old Victorian villa, vaguely Swiss-chalet design, with fretted-wood balconies and blue shutters. He glanced at his watch. Half past five. Tea was at six.

He entered a dim hallway furnished with a side-table holding an assortment of tourist brochures, a large brass bowl holding dusty pampas-grass, a carved chair, and an assortment of wellington boots. He pressed a bell on the wall and a door at the back of the wall opened and a thick, heavy-set man came towards him. He had blond hair and bright-blue eyes and a skin which had a strange high glaze on it, like china. Hamish thought he was probably in his fifties.

"You must be our Mr. Macbeth," he said breezily. "The name's Rogers, Harry Rogers. You'll find us one happy family here. Come upstairs and I'll show you and the doggie your room."

The room boasted none of the modern luxuries like telephone or television. But the bed looked comfortable, and through the window Hamish could see the grey line of the North Sea. "The bath-room's at the end of the corridor," said Mr. Rogers. "As you see, there's a wash-hand basin in the corner there. Tea's at six. Yes, none of this dinner business. Good old-fashioned high tea."

Hamish thanked him and Mr. Rogers left. Towser, tired after the long walk, crawled onto the bed and closed his eyes. Hamish quickly unpacked, taking out a bowl which he filled with water for the dog, and a can of dog food, a can opener, and another bowl. He filled the second bowl with the dog food and put it on the floor beside the water. Spoilt Towser did not like dog food, but, reflected Hamish, he would just need to put up with it for the duration of the holiday. Of course, maybe he could buy him some cold ham as a treat. Towser was partial to cold ham. He changed into a pair of jeans and a checked shirt, debated whether to wear a tie and decided against it, and then went downstairs and pushed open a door marked "Dining-Room." A small, birdlike woman, who turned out to be Mrs. Rogers, hailed him. "Mr. Macbeth, your table's here . . . with Miss Gunnery."

Hamish nodded to Miss Gunnery and sat down. All the other diners were already seated. Mr. Rogers appeared and introduced everyone to everyone else. Hamish's quick policeman's mind noted all the names and his sharp eyes took in the appearance of the other guests.

Miss Gunnery on the other side of the table had the sort of appearance which even in these modern days screamed spinster. She had a severe face, gold-rimmed glasses and a mouth like a trap. Her flat-chested figure was dressed despite the humidity of the day in a green tweed suit worn over a white shirt blouse.

At the next table was a man with his wife, a Mr.

and Mrs. Harris. Both were middle-aged. She had neatly permed brown hair and neat, closed features, and was dressed in a woollen sweater and cardigan and a black skirt. Her husband was wearing an open-necked shirt and a trendy black leather jacket and jeans, the sort of outfit that tired businessmen in a search for fading youth have taken to wearing, almost like a uniform. He was grey-haired, had large staring eyes and a bulbous nose.

Beyond them were Mr. and Mrs. Brett and their three children, Heather, Callum, and Fiona, aged seven, four, and three, respectively. Mr. Brett was a comfortable, chubby man with glasses and an air of benign stupidity. His wife was an artificial redhead with a petty face and pencilled eyebrows. Either they were plucked, a rare fashion these days, thought Hamish, or they had fallen off, or she had been born that way. She had pencilled in arches of eyebrows, which gave her a look of perpetual surprise.

At the window table were two girls called Tracey Fink and Cheryl Gamble, both from Glasgow. They both had hair sun-streaked by chemicals rather than sunlight and white pinched faces under a load of make-up, and both were wearing identical outfits, striped black-and-white sweaters and black ski pants with straps under the instep and dirty sneakers. And in a far corner was a solitary man who had the honour of having a table to himself. His name was Mr. Andrew Biggar. He had a tanned face and thick brown hair streaked with grey, small clever brown eyes, and a long, humorous mouth.

High tea, that famous Scottish meal now hardly ever served, consists of one main dish, usually cold ham, and salad and chips, washed down with tea. In the middle of each table was a cake stand. On the bottom were thin slices of white bread scraped with butter. On the next layer were scones and teacakes, and on the top, cakes filled with ersatz cream and covered in violently coloured icing.

"Grand day," said Hamish conversationally to Miss Gunnery, for every day in Scotland where it is not exactly freezing cold and pouring wet is designated a "grand day."

Her eyes snapped at him through her glasses. "Is it? I find it damp and overcast."

Hamish relapsed into a crushed silence. He wished he had not come. But Mr. Harris's voice rose above the conversation at the other tables, he of the trendy leather jacket, and caught Hamish's attention.

"Well, this holiday was your idea, Doris," he said.

"I only said the tea was a trifle weak," protested his wife.

"Always finding fault, that's your problem," said Mr. Harris. "If you exercised more and thought less about your stomach, you might be as fit as me."

"I only said—"

"You said. You said," he jeered. He looked around the room. "That's women for you. Always nitpicking."

"Bob, *please*," whispered his wife.

"Please what?"

"*You* know." She cast a scared look around the dining-room. "Everyone's listening."

"Let them listen. I'm not bound by your suburban little fears, my dear." His voice rose to a high falsetto. "What *will* the neighbours think."

And so he went on and on.

The severe Miss Gunnery, who prided herself on "keeping herself to herself," was driven to open her mouth and say to the tall, lanky, red-headed man opposite, "That fellow is a nag."

"Aye, the worst kind," agreed Hamish, and then smiled, and at that smile, Miss Gunnery thawed even more. "Mrs. Harris is right," she said. "The tea is disgustingly weak, the ham is mostly fat, and those cakes look vile. I know this place is cheap..."

"Maybe there's a fish-and-chip shop in the village," said Hamish hopefully. "I might take a walk there later. My dog likes fish and chips."

"Oh, you have a dog? What breed?"

"Towser's a mixture of every kind of breed."

Miss Gunnery looked amused. "Towser! I didn't think anyone called a dog Towser these days—or Rover, for that matter."

"It started as a wee bit o' a joke, that name," said Hamish, "and then the poor animal got stuck wi' it."

"What do you do for a living, Mr. Macbeth?"

The nag's voice had temporarily ceased. There was silence in the dining-room. "I'm a civil servant," said Hamish. He did not like telling people he was a policeman because they usually shrank away from him. And he had found that when he said he was a civil servant, it sounded so boring that no one ever asked him where he worked or in what branch of the organization.

"I'm a schoolteacher," said Miss Gunnery. "I've never been to Skag before. It seemed a good chance to get a cheap holiday."

"When did you arrive?"

"Today, like the rest. We're all the new intake."

Mr. Rogers and his wife hovered about among the tables, snatching away plates as soon as any diner looked as if he or she was finished. "We have television in the lounge across the hall," announced Mr. Rogers. His wife was carefully packing away uneaten cakes into a large plastic box. Hamish guessed, and as it turned out correctly, that they would make their appearance again during the following days until they had all either been eaten or gone stale.

The company moved through to the lounge. Bob Harris had temporarily given up baiting his wife, but Andrew Biggar made the mistake of asking Doris Harris what she would like to see.

"*Coronation Street* is just about to come on," said Doris shyly. "I would like to see that if no one else minds."

Her husband's voice cut across the murmur of assent. "Trust you to inflict your penchant for soaps on everyone else. How you can watch that pap is beyond me."

Hamish walked over to the television set, found "Coronation Street," and turned up the volume. "I like "Coronation Street,' " he lied to Doris. "Always watch it."

He sat down next to Miss Gunnery. He was aware of the nag's voice all through the programme, sneering and jeering at the characters. He sighed and looked about the room. The chairs were arranged in a half-circle in front of the television set. The fireplace was blocked up and a two-bar electric heater stood in front of it. There was a set of bookshelves containing battered paperbacks, no doubt left behind by previous guests. The Rogerses were probably too mean to buy any. The chairs were upholstered in a scratchy fabric. The carpet was a worn-out green with faded yellow flowers. There were various dim pictures on the walls, Highland cattle in Highland mist, and a grim photograph of a Victorian lady who stared down on all. Probably the original owner, thought Hamish.

At the end of the programme, which he had only stayed to watch for Mrs. Harris's sake, he rose and said to Miss Gunnery, "I'm going to walk my dog along to the village and see if there's a fish-and-chips shop. Want to come?"

"I don't eat fish and chips," she said primly, looking down her nose.

The tetchiness that had been in him for months rose to the surface again. "So you prefer that high-class muck we had for tea?"

There was an edge of contempt to his light Highland voice and Miss Gunnery flushed. "I'm being silly," she said, getting to her feet. "I'd enjoy the walk."

Hamish went up to get Towser, but when he descended to the hall again it was to find not only Miss Gunnery waiting for him but the rest of the party, with the exception of the Harrises.

They did not say anything like "We've decided to come too," but merely fell into line behind the policeman like obedient children being taken for a walk.

Mr. Brett was the first to break the silence. "A stone's throw from the sea," he exclaimed. "You would need to have a strong arm to throw a stone that distance."

"Are ye sure there's a chip shop, Jimmy?" asked Cheryl. She hailed from Glasgow, where everyone was called Jimmy, or so it seemed, if you listened to the inhabitants.

"I don't know," said Hamish. "May be something in the pub."

"I'm starving," confided Tracey, stooping to pat Towser. "I could eat a horse between two bread vans."

Cheryl slapped her playfully on the back and both girls giggled.

"It's a pity little Mrs. Harris couldn't come as well," said Andrew Biggar. "Don't suppose she gets much fun. Are you in the army, by any chance, Mr. Macbeth?"

"Hamish. I'm called Hamish. No, Andrew. Civil servant. What makes ye say that?"

"When I first saw you, I thought you were

probably usually in uniform. Got it wrong. I'm an army man myself. Forcibly retired."

"Oh, those dreadful redundancies," said Miss Gunnery sympathetically. "And us so soon to be at war with Russia again."

"Don't say that," said Mrs. Brett, whose name turned out to be June, and her husband's, Dermott. "It's been a grim enough start. That man Harris should be shot."

"You can say that again," said Dermott Brett, so June predictably did and the couple roared with laughter at their own killing wit.

"I don't know if I'm going to be able to bear this holiday," murmured Miss Gunnery to Hamish.

"Och," said Hamish, who was beginning to feel better, "I think they're a nice enough bunch of people and there's nothing like a common resentment for banding people together." He winced remembering how common resentment had turned the villagers of Lochdubh against him.

"Harris, you mean," said Miss Gunnery. "But his voice does go on and on and it's not a very big place."

They arrived at the village of Skag. It consisted of rows of stone houses, some of them thatched, built on a point. The river Skag ran on one side of the point and on the other side was the broad expanse of the North Sea. The main street was cobbled but the little side streets were not surfaced and the prevalent white sand blew everywhere, dancing in little eddies on a rising breeze. "Getting fresher," said Hamish. "Look there. A bit of blue sky."

They walked down to the harbour and stood at the edge. The tide was coming in and the water sucked greedily at the wooden piles underneath them. Great bunches of seaweed rose and fell. Above them, the grey canopy rolled back until bright sunlight blazed down.

Hamish sniffed the air. "I smell fish and chips," he said, "coming from over there."

They set out after him and found a small fish-and-chips shop. Hamish suggested they walk to the beach and eat their fish and chips there.

They made their way with their packets past the other side of the harbour, where yachts were moored in a small basin, the rising wind humming and thrumming in the shrouds. There was a sleazy café overlooking the yacht basin, still open but empty of customers, the lights of a fruit machine winking in the gloom inside.

A path led round the back of the café, past rusting abandoned cars and fridges, old sofas and broken tables, to a rise of shingle and then down to where the shingle ended and the long white beach began.

"You spoil that dog," said Miss Gunnery as Hamish placed a fish supper on its cardboard tray down in front of Towser.

Hamish did not reply. He knew he spoilt Towser but did not like anyone to comment on the fact.

"Why does a woman like Doris marry a pillock like that?" asked Andrew Biggar.

June Brett nudged her chubby husband playfully in the ribs. "They're all saints before you marry them and then the beast comes out."

Dermott Brett snarled at her and his wife shrieked with delight. Faces could be misleading, thought Hamish. June looked rather petty and mean when she was not speaking, but when she did, she became transformed into a good-natured woman. The Brett children were making sandcastles down by the water. They were remarkably well behaved. Heather, the seven-year-old, was looking after her young brother and toddling sister, making sure the little Fiona did not wander into the water. Long ribbons of white sand snaked along the harder damp surface of the sand underneath and then there came a haunting humming sound.

"Whit's that?" cried Cheryl, clutching Tracey.

"Singing sands," said Hamish. "I remember hearing there were singing sands here but I forgot about it."

"It's eerie," said Miss Gunnery. "In fact, the whole place is a bit odd. It never gets dark this time of year, does it, Hamish?"

He shook his head, thinking that the place was indeed eerie. Because of the bank of shingle behind the beach and the flatness of the land behind, there was a feeling of being cut off from the rest of the world. He remembered the seer's prediction with a shudder and then his common sense took over. Angus had heard the gossip about his holiday and had invented death and trouble to pay Hamish back for having called him a fraud.

Miss Gunnery was carefully collecting everyone's fish-and-chip papers when Hamish heard Dermott Brett say, "He's got worse."

"Who?" asked Andrew, lazily scraping in the sand for shells.

"Bob Harris."

"You know him?" asked Hamish.

"Yes, he was here last year."

Miss Gunnery paused in her paper-gathering. "You mean you stayed here and *came back!*"

"New management," said Dermott Brett. "It was owned by a couple of old biddies. They did a good tea, but their prices were quite high for a boarding-house. We weren't going to come back, because with the three kids it was coming to quite a bit. Then June saw the ad with the new cheap prices, but it said nothing about new management."

"What happened to the old women who owned it?" asked Hamish, ever curious.

"They were the Blane sisters, the Misses Blane. Rogers said they took a small house for themselves in Skag. Might call on them, if I can find them."

"So Harris is worse now?" pursued Hamish.

"He was bad enough last year, but in fits and starts. Didn't go on like he does now the whole time. Maybe he'll have settled down by tomorrow. Doris Harris wanted to come with us, but he ranted on at her when you were upstairs getting your dog about wasting good money on fish and chips when she had already eaten."

There was a scream of delight from the Brett children. Heather had placed the three-year-old Fiona on Towser's back. Towser was standing patiently, looking puzzled, his eyes rolling in Hamish's direction for help.

"Leave him be," shouted Hamish. Heather obediently lifted Fiona off Towser's back and Towser lolloped up the beach and lay panting at Hamish's feet.

"Time I got those kids in bed," said June. "They've been on the train all day."

"Come far?" asked Hamish.

"From London."

Dermott got to his feet and brushed sand from his trousers. He walked up to the children and swung the toddler onto his shoulders. June joined him, and the family set off together in the direction of the boarding-house.

"That's a nice family," said Miss Gunnery, returning from a rubbish bin on the other side of the shingle, where she had put the papers. "Perhaps we should be getting back as well."

"Whit aboot the night-life o' Skag?" sniggered Cheryl. "Me and Tracey'd like a drink."

"How old are you?" demanded Miss Gunnery severely.

Cheryl tossed her long blonde hair. "Old enough," she said. Her heavily made-up eyes flirted at Hamish. "Aye, old enough fur anything, isn't that right, Tracey?"

"Sure is," said Tracey in a dreadful imitation American accent. "So let's just mosey along to the pub."

"Bound to be bottled beer up here," said Andrew, "but I'm willing to try it. What about you, Hamish?"

"As long as they'll let Towser in."

"He's married tae his dug!" shrieked Cheryl.

Hamish's thin, sensitive face flushed angrily. He was ashamed of his affection for his dog, ashamed sometimes of Towser's yellowish mongrel appearance.

"I think a drink's just what we all need," said Andrew quickly. "Come along, Hamish."

Hamish had a sudden desire to sulk. But Miss Gunnery said, "I saw the pub near the harbour. It looked quite pretty. I think I'll go after all." She linked a bony arm in Hamish's as he stood up and the small party set off.

It was a pretty thatched pub with tubs of flowers at the door, more like an English inn than a Scottish one. But inside it was as plastic and dreary as the worst of Scottish pubs. A juke-box blared in the corner and a spotty moron was operating the fruit machine with monotonous regularity, his mouth hanging open as he fed in the coins. Hamish had noticed a table and chairs outside and suggested they take their drinks there. Cheryl and Tracey had rums and Coke, Miss Gunnery, a gin and tonic, Andrew, a bottle of beer, and Hamish, a whisky and a bag of potato crisps for Towser.

"There's a carnival here tomorrow," said Hamish. "Sideshows and everything. I saw a poster about it on the pub wall."

"I didn't see a fairground," said Andrew.

"It'll be here tomorrow all right," said Hamish, wise in the ways of Highland gypsies. "They come in the night like a medieval army and the next day, there they all are."

They finished their drinks and walked slowly back to the boarding-house. Cheryl and Tracey had decided to compete for the attention of Hamish Macbeth and so they walked arm in arm with him while Miss Gunnery and Andrew followed behind.

When they went into the boarding-house, Hamish collected a couple of paperbacks from the book-shelves in the lounge and went up the stairs to his room.

It was then that he found out that the Harrises had the room next door. Bob Harris's voice rose and fell, going on and on and on, punctuated by an occasional whimper from his wife.

Hamish wondered whether to go next door and tell the man to shut up, but as a policeman he had found out the folly of interfering in marital problems. Doris would probably round on him and tell him to leave her husband alone.

Or rather, that's what the lazy Hamish Macbeth told himself.

VISIT US ONLINE AT

WWW.HACHETTEBOOKGROUP.COM

FEATURES:

**OPENBOOK BROWSE AND
SEARCH EXCERPTS**

•

AUDIOBOOK EXCERPTS AND PODCASTS

•

AUTHOR ARTICLES AND INTERVIEWS

•

**BESTSELLER AND PUBLISHING
GROUP NEWS**

•

SIGN UP FOR E-NEWSLETTERS

•

**AUTHOR APPEARANCES AND TOUR
INFORMATION**

•

SOCIAL MEDIA FEEDS AND WIDGETS

•

DOWNLOAD FREE APPS

Bookmark Hachette Book Group
@ www.HachetteBookGroup.com